# TREASURE ISLAND

*By – Robert Louis Stevenson*

GOPU BOOKS
An Imprint of V&S PUBLISHERS

*Published by:*

V&S PUBLISHERS
VALUE & SUBSTANCE

**Head Office**
F-2/16, Ansari Road, Daryaganj,
New Delhi-110002 ☎ 23240026, 27, 28
✉ info@vspublishers.com
www.vspublishers.com

**Regional Office**
5-1-707/1, Brij Bhawan (Beside Central Bank of India Lane) Bank Street, Koti,
Hyderabad - 500 095 ☎ 040-24737290
✉ vspublishershyd@gmail.com

**Online Brandstore: amazon.in/vspublishers**

**Buy Books Online:** amazon • Flipkart | **Follow us on:**



ISBN 978-93-579421-5-7
**New Edition**

**Cataloging in Publication Data--DK**
Courtesy: D.K. Agencies (P) Ltd. <docinfo@dkagencies.com>

**Stevenson, Robert Louis**, 1850-1894, **author**.
Treasure island / by Robert Louis Stevenson. -- New edition. pages cm
Adventurous juvenile novel.
ISBN 9789357942157

1. Buried treasure--Juvenile fiction. 2. Pirates--Juvenile fiction. 3. Caribbean Area--History--18th century--Juvenile fiction. 4. Adventure stories, English. 5. Children's stories, English. I. Title.

LCC PZ7.S74Tr 2022 | DDC 823.8 23



***Printed at :*** Param Offsetters, Okhla, New Delhi–110020

# Contents

# Publisher's Note

In line with our thinking to make students, teens, young and other interested readers become familiar with the rich and popular classics of yesteryears, we have before you, a story retold in a language understood by them - the story of Treasure Island - in the shape of a graded reader book.

Treasure Island has been written by Robert Luis Stevenson in the later part of the 18th century is considered one of the first adventure stories specifically for adolescents with devoid of any emphasis on teaching morals.

It is so because a graded reader book is an 'easy reading' book specially created for children or learners of English as a second or other foreign languages. These are simplified and adapted versions of existing works. The language is graded for vocabulary, complexity of grammar structures and also by the number of words. They are made to cater to all levels from beginners through to advanced.

To simplify understanding the book, glossary has been given at the end of each chapter. Comprehension questions of different types are also gives at the end of the book as a special feature for a letter learning experience.

This book will help you remember vocabulary better and make studying fun, besides helping you go for extensive reading, that is, reading for pleasure outside the classroom.

We hope you will enjoy reading this unique piece of work. Feel free to write to us for any feedback.

# Introduction

The protagonist of Treasure Island, Jim Hawkins, has been asked by his friends Doctor Livesey and Squire Trelawney to narrate his experiences at the Treasure Island. Jim begins his recollections: at that time young Jim lived at his parents' inn, Admiral Benbow, near Bristol, England, in the eighteenth century. One day, an old and ragged-looking sea captain called Billy Bones comes to stay at the inn. The captain spent much of the time drinking rum, and after a pirate named Black Dog came to see him, he was so nervous that he had a fainting fit. Afterwards, he told Jim that Black Dog was after something kept in his sea chest: if he would ever die, he told Jim, the boy would find what was in it and follow the instructions inside.

A few days later, Billy Bones died in the inn after being presented with a black spot, or official pirate verdict of guilt or judgment. Jim and his mother unlocked Billy Bones' sea chest, finding some money, a journal, and a map. Their family friend and doctor, Dr. Livesey, deduced that the map was of an island where the pirate Flint buried a vast treasure. The district Squire, Trelawney, proposed that they buy a ship and go after the treasure, taking Livesey as ship's doctor and Jim as a cabin boy.

That is how the adventures of the Treasure Island began.

*The Treasure Island* was written by Scottish author Robert Louis Stevenson. The book was first published in 1883. Stevenson was born into a family that expected him to continue the family profession of civil engineering. But his ill health kept him from pursuing his studies and instead he began to write, beginning by writing a number of books about travelling through Europe and the United States. He married an American woman called Fanny Osborne whom he had met in France, and it is said that he wrote

*The Treasure Island* for his stepson Llyod Osborne. The idea for *The Treasure Island* came from a map of an imaginary island Stevenson drew with Lloyd. Stevenson took this map and decided to write a story for boys. Stevenson focussed almost entirely on plot in this book where lots of interesting things happen, and paid little attention to the writing style. Also, there are no major descriptions of characters.

Stevenson originally published *The Treasure Island* under the title *The Sea-Cook* in the magazine *Young Folks* over a period of several months from 1881 to 1882. It didn't do that well as a series of episodes. But then Stevenson repackaged the story as a book,*The Treasure Island,* in 1883, and it became a bestseller, gripping young readers even today.

# Main Characters

## Jim Hawkins

Jim Hawkins is the protagonist of Treasure Island. He is merely a boy when the events of the story take place. From a young age, Jim is used to manage responsibilities at Admiral Benbow, an inn owned by his ailing father. He is full of curiosity and the initial thoughts on an adventure out at sea excite him immensely. However, he soon learns that he is still not quite prepared for the adventures that await him on board the *Hispaniola*. Jim, however, is naturally clever and quick-witted: he is able to think fast and hide from danger when he needs to. But at the same time he is rebellious and is not able to stick to duty on various occasions. He does realize his mistakes later and tends to feel guilty about breaking the rules. He is special in many ways, yet not superhuman. He is like any boy of his age, who goes through all kinds of feelings such as fear, excitement, confusion, and guilt.

## Dr. Livesey

Dr. Livesey is a family friend of Jim's parents. He is the one who takes care of Jim's father until he passes away. He is dutiful and resourceful, making him a point of contact for Jim in case of any trouble. He is one of the first to recognize the significance of the treasure map. He, along with Squire Trelawney, arranges for the ship and the crew in order to sail for the treasure. The doctor is an intelligent man, loyal to those who are loyal to him. He too is fascinated with the idea of wealth and adventure that motivates so many characters in the book. He thinks of pirates as low and murderous creatures, and has no sympathy for them. Meanwhile, he is almost a father-figure for Jim, looking out for him at every step, even when Jim disappoints him.

## Squire Trelawney

A good friend of Dr. Livesey, Squire Trelawney is a good-hearted guy, extremely patriotic, and generous. He, along with Dr. Livesey, unveils the treasure map, and it is the Squire who tells everyone just how frightening and powerful Flint was. Squire Trelawney doesn't think much and is the one who gets everyone in trouble. He is the one who puts up the money for the voyage, and he's the one who (accidentally) hires a crew of pirates. He has a tendency to gossip, and sort of gives away the news about the treasure, which results in Silver and the other disloyal pirates becoming crew on the ship.

### Silver

John Long Silver is a cunning and sly pirate, who enters the ship as a cook, and brings along his team of nasty and notorious pirates. He has lost his leg in some kind of battle when he was part of Flint's group of buccaneers. He is represented as someone even dreaded men such as Billy Bones (the one-legged man) and Flint was scared of. He is able to initially charm Jim, Squire Trelawney and even Dr. Livesey, who are unable to see his true intentions. Soon, though, it becomes clear that Silver is evil and manipulating. He cares more than anything else about ensuring his own survival, and will do whatever it takes to save himself—even if that means betraying one group, then turning around and betraying another.

### Captain Smollett

Captain Smollett hired by Squire Trelawney to head the Hispaniola, is all about duty and discipline. He senses from the beginning something wrong with the crew and his suspicion of the voyage. Although the Squire and Jim despise him initially for his strict nature and for finding fault with a seemingly amicable crew, the Captain is proved right soon. The Captain insisted on rules and regulations at all times, and anyone found neglecting duty or breaking rules was sure to be pulled up by him. Sometimes, because of his insistence on rules, the Captain failed to see the value of practical solutions which employ a bit of cunningness.

### Ben Gunn

Formerly a member of Flint's crew, Ben Gunn is a marooned sailor whom Jim Hawkins meets on the island. Unlike the other pirates, Ben Gunn is not wicked and murderous. He is a survivor, who against all odds, manages to live for three years on the island by himself, killing and preserving goat meat and looking tirelessly for Flint's treasure. And he even manages to find it! He is considered slightly crazy by all, probably from living alone for so long. He is afraid of the other pirates, specially Silver. Meanwhile, Gunn is so grateful to have met Jim and found him friendly that he pledges full loyalty from his side.

# PART I
# THE OLD BUCCANEER

# 1 The Old Sea-Dog at the "Admiral Benbow"

At the **behest** of Squire Trelawney, Dr. Livesey, and a few others, young Jim Hawkins begins to narrate his adventures on the Treasure Island. Jim decides to record every detail of what took place, but omits mentioning the island's exact location, as he believes that a part of treasure still lies buried there.

The story begins with Jim recounting his first meeting with an old sailor called Billy Bones. Asking to be addressed as the "Captain", this large, **ragged** man walked into Admiral Benbow one day, an inn owned by Jim's ailing father. Carrying a mysterious chest and many marks of war, the Captain came seeking a quiet and out-of-the-way place to live in, and found Admiral Benbow, **overlooking** the sea, to be just that. The old sailor doled out a few gold coins and self-appointedly moved in, eventually staying for far longer than his payment covered.

A silent man by custom, the Captain spent his days walking the cliffs and observing the sea through his brass telescope. His evenings meant drinking lots and lots of rum and singing his **sea-chanty**:

"Fifteen men on the dead man's chest -Yo-ho-ho, and a bottle of rum!"

His raucous drinking and coarse singing often frightened the other inmates. On some days, the drunken Captain would terrorise everyone else to join in the singing of his violent sea songs and then listen to his **dismaying** accounts of wicked men, dreadful storms, and grim life. Jim's father worried that the inn would be doomed as the people would cease coming owing to the Captain's **preposterous** disposition. But Jim believed the Captain's presence was in fact good, bringing some excitement into the boring, quiet country-life. It was the **notoriety** of the Captain that attracted customers and he even earned some admiration from younger locals who considered him a "real old salt".

Not just notoriety, there was enough mystery surrounding the Captain as well. He was always dressed in rough filthy clothes and never spent a penny. Throughout his stay he never received or sent a letter, never spoke to anyone but the neighbours (mostly when drunk on rum), and his great sea-chest was always locked. Meanwhile, the Captain himself was wary of a **seafaring** man coming after him and checked out any seaman visiting Admiral Benbow with utmost caution before making himself public. He made Jim his **confidante** and promised him a small fee every month if Jim kept his "weather-eye open for a seafaring man with one leg", and alerted the Captain the moment one such appeared.

One evening Dr. Livesey was at the inn, attending to Jim's father's deteriorating health. At this time, the **inebriated** Captain broke into his sailor song in full blast, banging the desk alongside, in a manner that would mean a quiet submission for all around.

"Fifteen men on the dead man's chest—
Yo-ho-ho, and a bottle of rum!
Drink and the devil had done for the rest—
Yo-ho-ho, and a bottle of rum!"

Dr. Livesey, a stranger to this high drama of every evening in Admiral Benbow, did not oblige the Captain with his demand for silence while he roared, and kept his business and conversation alive. The Captain was angry and threatened the doctor. In response, Dr. Livesey calmly predicted that death would be near if the Captain did not stop drinking.

"...if you keep on drinking rum, the world will soon be quit of a very dirty scoundrel!"

These warnings further enraged the Captain who threatened the doctor with a knife. The **undeterred** doctor, who also happened to be a district law enforcement official, had the Captain subdue his rage after he warned that he'll have the Captain arrested if he kept threatening the people.

The Captain held his peace that evening, and for many evenings to come.

## Glossary

- behest : a person's order or command
- overlooking : have a view of
- sea-chanty : sailor's song
- ragged : old and torn
- dismaying : causing distress
- preposterous : contrary to reason or common sense
- notoriety : famous for some bad quality or deed
- seafaring : travelled a lot on sea
- confidante : a person with whom one shares a secret
- inebriated : drunk or intoxicated
- undeterred : not stopping despite setbacks

# 2 Black Dog Appears and Disappears

On a cold January morning soon after, the Captain was out on a stroll along the beach and Jim was readying the breakfast table for his return. A pale stranger, wearing a **cutlass** and missing two fingers on the left hand walked into the inn. Although curious looking, Jim made a quick note that this wasn't the "seafaring man with one leg". The stranger ordered some rum and asked Jim if his "mate Bill" was there at the inn. Jim, unaware of the Captain's real name (Billy Bones) until this point, at first refused to know any Bill, but as the stranger rightly pointed to a scar on the Captain's right cheek, Jim confirmed his lodging at the inn and said he is about to return soon.

The stranger kept hanging about in the inn, waiting impatiently for the Captain's return, **peering** around the corner like a cat waiting for a mouse. Sensing that this person may mean harm to the Captain, Jim tried to start out to warn the Captain before his return to the inn, but the strange man prevented him from leaving.

Pulling Jim behind the **parlour** in spite of his unwillingness, they both waited it out for the Captain. Soon the Captain approached, almost gasping as the stranger called out his name "Bill". Although **startled** as if a ghost had appeared the Captain did recognize this person and addressed him as "Black Dog".

Black Dog ordered rum for the Captain and himself, and bade Jim to leave them to talk and leave the door wide open --- so that he is able to escape when the time comes. The Captain and Black Dog launched into a long conversation. Meanwhile Jim failed to overhear them, in spite of his best efforts. Suddenly their conversation turned violent and Jim could hear the clashing of swords.

He rushed back in, to witness a lively sword fight; soon after Black Dog **retreated** with some wounds. Jim found the Captain in a state of great anger and ill-at-ease. He was eager to leave the inn and uttered the word "rum", but before Jim could get any, he collapsed on the floor with a loud noise.

Jim and his mother tried their best to revive the old man; to their relief Dr. Livesey walked in at that very moment on a visit to Jim's father. Dr. Livesey informed that the Captain had suffered a stroke. The doctor treated the Captain, assisted by Jim. As soon as he regained consciousness the Captain said the words "Black Dog", to be told that Black Dog had fled. Jim and Dr. Livesey **confined** the Captain to his bed and the doctor warned him yet again to not drink, if he wished to live.

**Glossary**

- cutlass : a short sword with a curved blade used by sailors
- peering : to look through a narrow space searchingly
- parlour : sitting room
- startled : sudden shock or alarm
- retreated : move away from enemies
- confined : restricted to a particular location

# 3 The Black Spot

Jim continued to look after the weakly and **bedfast** Captain. One afternoon as he brought him some cooling drinks and medicines, the Captain began to implore Jim to get him a swig of rum. But Jim decided to stick with Dr. Livesey's advice. The desperate Captain even offered money to Jim **coercing** him to **sidestep** the doctor's orders. An offended Jim said he does not want any money but what the Captain owes his father. The Captain's requests soon started getting louder, and Jim, worried about his father who was in a critical state decided to oblige the Captain.

As he greedily **gulped** down a glass of rum, the Captain asked Jim how long the doctor wanted him to stay in bed. He was shocked to hear that his confinement was to be of seven days and declared that that would be impossible. Slightly energized by the alcohol he tried to hurriedly get out of the bed, but found it difficult to move.

The Captain recounted to Jim that he was Captain Flint's first mate (second in command). Captain Flint, now dead, was a notorious pirate who had acquired a lot of wealth. The Captain told Jim that he was the only person who now knew where all of this treasures lied, and wouldn't mind sharing it with Jim if he agreed to help him out now. The Captain said to Jim that men like Black Dog and others who are worse, all former crew of Captain Flint's ship, wanted to steal the Captain's sea-chest. The Captain was very worried that they will give him the "black spot", a kind of secret pirate summons (signalling ....). He also instructed Jim to get Dr.

Livesey to call down the law upon these notorious seamen when they came. The Captain **ranted** some more in his **delirious** state, and then fell back asleep after having his medicine, leaving Jim to **ponder** upon a lot.

That night Jim's father, who had also been gravely ill, died. This unfortunate turn of event took Jim's mind off the Captain and his **impending** troubles. The next day the Captain came downstairs and poured himself some rum **liberally**, taking advantage of the **ensuing** crisis at the inn. This continued for a few days and the Captain drank without interference, growing weaker and weaker.

A day after his father's funeral Jim was standing at the door of the inn, his mind still full of grief. A **sinister**-looking, blind and disfigured man, almost in the **garb** of a beggar, walked up in front of inn. The scary figure after making sure he was at the right address grabbed Jim's hand and asked to be taken to the Captain. Jim tried to **dissuade** him at first, but the blind man gripped Jim's hand "like a vice" and threatened to break his arm if he did not obey. Jim was forced to take the **menacing** man to the drunken Captain, who turned pale at his sight, as if struck by some **mortal** sickness. The blind man handed over the dreaded "black spot" to the Captain and sneaked out of the inn, while the Captain and Jim were still reeling in shock of his evilness. A few minutes had passed before the Captain gathered his senses back and looked at what had been handed to him. It said "Ten o'clock!" ---the Captain cried out he had only six hours left and sprang to his feet. But such was the horror of the black spot that the Captain started **reeling**, and in a moment fell on the floor dead. He had suffered a second stroke.

Jim and his mother ran to his rescue but in vain. This was the second death Jim saw in a week and he burst into a flood of tears.

## Glossary

| | | |
|---|---|---|
| ➢ | bedfast | : bedridden |
| ➢ | coercing | : obtain something by force |
| ➢ | sidestep | : avoid |
| ➢ | gulped | : swallow quickly in large mouthfuls |
| ➢ | ranted | : speak in an impassioned way |
| ➢ | delirious | : disturbed state of mind |
| ➢ | ponder | : think about |
| ➢ | impending | : about to happen |
| ➢ | liberally | : generous or large amounts |
| ➢ | ensuing | : as a result of something |
| ➢ | sinister | : evil or criminal |
| ➢ | garb | : clothing |
| ➢ | dissuade | : persuade not to |
| ➢ | menacing | : threatening |
| ➢ | mortal | : something that can cause death |
| ➢ | reeling | : lose one's balance |

# 4 The Sea-Chest

Jim wasted no time in **divulging** every detail of the Captain's story to his mother: how the evil pirates plotted to take the Captain's sea chest. The mother and son realized that the Captain had left them in a **perilous** situation and every moment they spent in the inn thereafter they had their hearts in their mouths. Almost certain that the Captain's enemies could break into the inn any minute then, Jim and his mother decided to flee to the neighbouring village for help. Jim had seen two such wicked men himself, Black Dog and the blind beggar, and their very thoughts made him jump in his skin for terror.

Much to their disappointment, none of the people in the village were eager to help out the Hawkins. The villagers were **petrified** at the mention of the name Captain Flint or anyone associated with him. Not only did they hesitate to accompany Jim and his mother to the inn, they strictly advised against them returning to the inn as well. Several were willing to ride to Dr. Livesey to have him arrange for lawful protection, but that was in the opposite direction of the inn.

Meanwhile, despite the warnings of the villagers, Mrs Hawkins was determined to return to the inn and get hold of some money from the Captain's chest: as much as was owed to them as rent, not a penny more.

"She would not, she declared, lose money that belonged to her fatherless boy;"

And so armed with a loaded pistol offered by one of the villagers, Jim, left with no choice accompanied his mother to the inn, ignoring the villagers' cries at their foolhardiness.

Back at the inn Jim **reluctantly** searched the pockets and the dead body of the Captain for the keys to the chest, his heart pounding, all the while fearing the arrival of the blind man. Finding the key around the Captain's neck, Jim and his mother hurriedly opened up the chest and examined its contents. The chest contained apart from some fresh, unworn clothes "a quadrant, a tin cannikin, several sticks of tobacco, two braces of very handsome pistols, a piece of bar silver, an old Spanish watch and some other trinkets of little value and mostly of foreign make, a pair of compasses mounted with brass, and five or six curious West Indian shells." At last, they found hidden at the bottom of the chest a bag of gold coins of many different countries, of which Jim's mother wanted to separate her dues. But because she could recognize only English guineas, and since the honest Mrs Hawkins wouldn't take a farthing more than was her due, she was extremely slow to count them.

Half-way through the **tedious** counting process, Jim heard the tapping of the blind man's stick approaching towards the inn. Mrs Hawkins grabbed what she had counted and Jim quickly got hold of some papers wrapped in an oil-cloth that he found in the chest, and in the dark they ran out of the inn, both scared out of their wits.

"I'll take what I have," she said, jumping to her feet. "And I'll take this to square the count," said I, picking up the oilskin packet.

In a moment, they were in full retreat. But before they could get very far, to Jim's dismay, overcome by fear Mrs Hawkins started to feel weak and fainted. Jim managed to pull her under the arch of the nearby bridge, out of sight but "within earshot of the inn".

**Glossary**

- divulging : give out information
- perilous : dangerous or risky
- petrified : so frightened that one is unable to move
- reluctantly : unwillingly
- tedious : tiresome

# 5 The Last of the Blind Man

Terrified he was, but curiosity got the better of him and Jim started looking out of his hiding place, as a bunch of notorious pirates **ransacked** the inn. Even through the distance and the mist, Jim could make out that one of these men was the infamous blind man and he seemed to be the one in command, **hurling** abuses and orders at the others.

The men rushed into Admiral Benbow and were shocked to see the Captain dead. They shouted back to the blind man, "Bill's dead." Here Jim learned that the blind man was called Pew. The merciless seamen cared two hoots about the dead Captain and continued their single-minded **quest** for "treasure", searching the Captain's body and his opened up chest. They looked disappointed to find money in the chest, clearly indicating that they were after something more precious that had been kept in the chest and that belonged to Captain Flint: and that which was now gone. Pew immediately guesses that whatever they wanted was with Jim and showed regret for not having poked Jim's eyes out at their first encounter.

Pew ordered his motley crew to "scatter and find" Jim and his mother. Then followed destruction of the inn: breaking of furniture, smashing of contents, ransacking of property. As the search yielded no result, Pew started to scream at his men, angering them and they all engaged in violent quarrel thereafter. In the midst of this **kerfuffle** a pistol shot was heard in the distance and the men began to panic, scattering here and there. Soon after, noise of policemen arriving on horses was heard. The pirates ran for their lives. Everyone managed to escape, except blind Pew, who was left behind by his comrades.

From his hiding Jim noticed that the boy who had gone to get Dr. Livesey had returned with some revenue officers, whom he must have met on the way. Jim hailed the boy for showing presence of mind in getting the officers, as Dr. Livesey was farther away. The officers reached the inn to find the pirates gone and the inn ransacked beyond description. However, Pew mistakenly ran into the path of the officers, fell under their horses' hooves and was killed.

Now sure he was out of harm's way Jim sprang out of his hideout and went up to the officers. They helped carry Mrs Hawkins to the village where she was looked after and regained consciousness. Jim recounted the incidents of that day to the officer who seemed to be in command, Mr Dance. Jim also disclosed the fact that what the robbers were after may actually be with him --- the oilcloth-wrapped papers in his pocket. Jim was, however, reluctant to hand these troubled papers to Mr Dance. Jim said he would prefer to show the papers to Dr. Livesey, and he then set off with Mr Dance's party for Dr. Livesey's house.

### Glossary

- ransacked : go through a place stealing objects and causing damage
- hurling : to throw out
- quest : search for something
- kerfuffle : commotion or fuss

# 6 The Captain's Papers

Jim arrived at the house of Dr. Livesey with Mr. Dance and his men, eager to let the doctor in on his secrets. Here they learned that the doctor was at Squire Trelawney's house. Jim and Mr. Dance proceeded to the Squire's house, where the two men were in conversation around a bright fire, their pipes in hand.

Jim took a moment to observe Squire Trelawney closely: he was big man, his face reddened and lined from his long travels, and he seemed to have a quick and high temper, but not bad.

Mr Dance did not waste a minute to blurt out the whole story, while the two men sat there listening, often surprised and always full of interest. The doctor and the Squire **lauded** Jim's mother's courage in going back to the inn for her dues. As Mr Dance ended his account, the Squire praised the officer and Jim as well for their deeds. Dr. Livesey, however, was more interested in going through the contents of the oil-skin packet that Jim had possessed, but he waited to open it until after Mr Dance left the building and Jim had had a hearty dinner.

Before they proceeded to open the packet, Squire Trelawney described the pirate Flint as the "bloodthirstiest buccaneer that sailed". According to the Squire, Blackbeard was a child in comparison to Flint, and that Flint had acquired great deal of wealth over the years. The Squire vowed that if the packet Jim brought had clues to where Flint's treasure lied, then he would outfit a ship to find it.

With Jim's permission Dr. Livesey then opened up the packet. It contained a book and a sealed paper. The book contained listings of various sums of money and dates covering over twenty years. While the doctor and Jim drew a blank, the Squire comfortably explained that these were records of all the ships sunk and towns plundered by Flint and his notorious crew; and the amounts were the share of **plunder** acquired by Captain Billy Bones in each place. As the amounts entered into his account book went up, Billy Bones rose in rank.

After reviewing the book, the three then went onto open up the sealed paper. The doctor opened up the seals with great care and there fell out the map of an island about 45 square miles in area. This island was the location of the buried treasure: shaped like a fat dragon standing on its hind legs, the "Treasure Island" was marked with three crosses in red ink, one labeled "bulk of treasure here." Over the back of the map was **scribbled** some hand-written instructions:

> *Tall tree, Spy-glass shoulder, bearing a point to the N. of N.N.E. Skeleton Island E.S.E. and by E.*
>
> *Ten feet.*
>
> *The bar silver is in the north cache; you can find it by the trend of the east hummock, ten fathoms south of the black crag with the face on it.*
>
> *The arms are easy found, in the sand-hill, N. point of north inlet cape, bearing E. and a quarter N.*
>
> *J.F.*

These lines read Greek to Jim, but the doctor and the Squire were brimming with joy at what they had laid their hands upon, and began their planning of reaching for this treasure. Squire Trelawney proposed to leave for the port city of Bristol immediately, where he would obtain a ship and hire a crew. Dr. Livesey was to sail as the ship's doctor, Jim as the cabin boy, and three other men whom the Squire named (Redruth, Joyce, and Hunter) were to come along. The group would sail in search of the island and the treasure. Meanwhile Dr. Livesey warned the Squire to not **utter** a word about their plan to another soul; Squire Trelawney promised to remain "silent as the grave."

## Glossary

- lauded : praise highly
- plunder : loot
- scribbled : write or draw hurriedly
- utter : say

# PART II
# THE SEA-COOK

# 7 I go to Bristol

Weeks had passed since Squire Trelawney had set off for Bristol. The Squire was busy breaking ground to get their voyage on sail, while Dr. Livesey was in London to hand over the charge of his practice to another physician. Meanwhile, Jim waited with baited breath and "full of sea dreams" for the anticipated adventures to unfold. Threat loomed large over Jim for possessing the much wanted treasure map and so he was staying at the Squire's **mansion** under the good care of old Tom Redruth, the Squire's trusted servant and head gamekeeper. In his imagination Jim had already travelled to the island and "explored every acre of its surface". He **envisaged** the island to be sometimes "thick with savages with whom we fought, sometimes full of dangerous animals that hunted us". However, in reality the adventures were to exceed Jim's expectations in both strangeness and tragedy.

One fine day then a letter from the Squire arrived. Originally addressed to Dr. Livesey, the letter also bore the permission for Jim to open it in the doctor's absence. The letter informed that Squire Trelawney had bought a **schooner** called *Hispaniola,* which was ready to sail. The Squire described his meeting with an old sailor, a fellow named Long John Silver, who had lost a leg in war. The one-legged sailor missed the sea and wished to sail again.The Squire was touched by his story and hired him as the ship's cook. Silver in turn helped the Squire find a suitable crew for the ship. Squire Trelawney desired Jim and Dr. Livesey to join him forthwith in Bristol.

The next day Jim visited Admiral Benbow accompanied by Redruth. The place looked much different from the last time Jim was there. The Captain was gone, the Squire had got everything repaired, and his mother was in good health and spirit. Jim spent the day with his mother before bidding her a sad farewell and setting off for Bristol the next morning by stage, yet again in Redruth's company.

It was an overnight journey and Jim had **dozed off**. He opened his eyes to find himself in Bristol. They walked up to the inn where the Squire was staying and were greeted by Squire Trelawney. Dr. Livesey too had arrived the night before.

On the one hand Jim was full of "delightful dreams" of the sea, and on the other hand Squire Trelawney too was soaked up in the romance of it all: he had dressed himself in a sea-officer's **attire** and imitated a sailor's walk.

The Squire declared that the party would set sail the next day.

**Glossary**

- mansion : a large and impressive-looking house
- envisaged : to imagine what might happen in the future
- schooner : a sailing ship that has at least two masts
- dozed off : to sleep
- attire : clothes, usually formal wear

# 8 At the Sign of the Spy-glass

The next morning Jim met John Silver. Squire Trelawney asked Jim to take a letter to Silver whom he would find at the Spyglass, a **tavern** he owns in the town. Jim was happy to run this **errand** as it meant walking past ships and seas. He found the place easily enough: it was a "bright little place" with a newly painted sign, neat red curtains, and a cleanly sanded floor. The ones inside were mostly seafaring men, whose loud banter scared Jim and he hesitated a few moments before making an entry.

Now from the moment Jim had read the Squire's letter, he had been suspicious about Silver being the same one-legged man that Captain Billy Bones had asked him to watch out for. However, his doubts began to **dwindle** as he saw the man in front of him. Silver was easy to spot: Jim saw the one-legged sailor moving about the inn with a crutch under his left shoulder, a plain face, and a cheerful disposition. He managed himself with wonderful**d exterity**, almost hopping "like a bird", his missing leg not impairing his strength and mobility. Silver seemed far removed from the likes of the buccaneers Jim had met so far: the Captain, Black Dog and the **ominous** Pew. Jim instantly liked him and decided to trust him.

Jim introduced himself to Silver and Silver loudly announced to everyone in the inn that Jim was their "new cabin boy". The sight of Jim aroused some anxiety in one of customers seated at the inn, who quickly began to leave. Jim identified this person as Black Dog and shouted to stop him as he was on the run by now. Acting upon Jim's concerns Silver sent out two men after him. Silver claimed to not know Black Dog, but vouched that he had seen him at the inn several times with a blind beggar called Pew. The men returned saying they had lost track of Black Dog in the crowd.

Silver apologized to Jim for not having caught the **scoundrel**. For a moment Jim was again skeptical of Silver having a connection with the evil pirates. But Silver's disappointment at Black Dog's escape and letting down Jim, and the negative view of these men he shared with Jim, convinced Jim of his honesty and cleanliness yet again.

Silver charmed Jim with his smooth talk and natural liveliness. They strolled back to the inn walking down the docks as Silver further impressed the sea-struck Jim with his knowledge of the ships, sharing **anecdotes** about seamen and teaching him **nautical** phrases. Jim felt that Silver was "the best of possible shipmates".

At the inn, Silver narrated the whole incident to the Squire and the doctor "with a great deal of spirit and the most perfect truth."Everyone agreed that it was shame that Black Dog had escaped but nothing could to be done about it. Silver departed after this account and the three others set off to see the ship. It must be mentioned here that Silver's honesty and **benevolence** had rubbed off on Dr. Livesey as well and he went on to say to the Squire:"I don't put much faith in your discoveries, as a general thing; but I will say this, John Silver suits me."

**Glossary**

- tavern : an inn or a pub
- errand : a task that you do for another person that usually involves going somewhere
- dwindle : to become less or smaller
- dexterity : skill to perform tasks, usually with the hands
- ominous : a suggestion that something bad will happen in the future
- scoundrel : a dishonest person
- anecdotes : an interesting and short story about a real person or incident
- nautical : something connected to sailors, sailing, and ships
- benevolence : the quality of being helpful and kind

# 9 Powder and Arms

As soon as Jim, Dr. Livesey, and Squire Trelawney boarded the *Hispaniola,* they ran into Mr Arrow, the ship's first mate. Arrow was a brown, old sailor "with earrings in his ears and a **squint**." The next person to walk up to us was Captain Smollett. Jim at once noticed that while the Squire spoke very warmly to Arrow, he did not seem to have much regard for the Captain Smollett.

The Captain seemed to be an **upright** and **plainspoken** person who had a lot to say about the matters of the ship.The Squire did not seem to be much interested in what the Captain had to say. But since Dr. Livesey was ready to lend a patient ear, Captain Smollett sounded off his opinion about the whole venture, even at the risk of offending some.

The Captain did not trust many of the crew: men hired by John Silver, rather than the Captain as it ought to have been his right. He did not approve of the habit of first mate Arrow of associating too freely with the common sailors. The Captain was brought onboard on "sealed orders": the ship was to sail on a secret mission and the Captain's duty was to sail it to any place he was asked to. However, the Captain had now noticed and especially disliked the fact that the whole crew knew they were sailing for treasure, while the Captain hadn't been told.The Captain said that the crew knew about the bearings of the island, the existence of a treasure map and even the red crosses on the map. The Captain **cautioned** that while treasure voyages are risky to start with, such **abundant** knowledge about their voyage made it doubly so.

Though there was no concrete proof of the Captain's cynicism, he insisted that the Squire and his mates remain guarded. Dr. Livesey agreed with the Captain calling his concerns genuine. He assured him that they were aware of what lied ahead and were ready to take a calculated risk; they were determined to stick to the plan. Having so heard, the duty-bound Captain suggested a few changes in arrangements for the safety of the Squire and his mates. He asked that Squire Trelawney's servants, Redruth and others whom the Squire had brought along, be quartered near the Squire's cabin rather than before the mast with the rest of the crew. He wanted the store of guns and powder be removed from the **forehold** and be kept below the cabin. Dr. Livesey observed that these arrangements would effectively separate the newly hired crewmen from the Squireand his men, as well as from the weapons. Asked if he feared a **mutiny**, the Captain answered that he was only being cautious as he was "responsible for the ship's safety and the life of every man aboard of her." The Captain also warned that the treasure map be **safeguarded** from all including Arrow and himself.

Squire Trelawney agreed to do as the Captain pleased but maintained that the Captain's conduct was "unmanly, unsailorly, and downright un-English." Dr. Livesey believed that the Captain was the second of the Squire's good finds; the first being Silver. The doctor seemed to trust both the men completely.

Later that day, everyone got busy shifting the powder and the berths, when Silver came onboard. Surprised by the changes, Silver almost objected calling it wastage of time. The Captain was, however, not in a mood to listen and sent Silver down to the kitchen, followed by Jim who was instructed by the Captain to help Silver prepare the meals. On his way down Jim heard the Captain tell the doctor of him, "I'll have no favorites on my ship!", as he was clearly treated by Silver as a pet.

After the first **encounter**, Jim felt he was more on the Squire's side and hated Captain Smollett "deeply."

## Glossary

| | | |
|---|---|---|
| ➢ squint | : | to look at something with your eyes partly closed |
| ➢ upright | : | a person standing or sitting with their back straight |
| ➢ plainspoken | : | blunt or outspoken |
| ➢ cautioned | : | to say something as a warning |
| ➢ abundant | : | something available in large quantities |
| ➢ forehold | : | the foreword part of the hold of a ship |
| ➢ mutiny | : | a rebellion usually by soldiers against the authorities |
| ➢ safeguarded | : | keeping somebody or something safe |
| ➢ encounter | : | to meet someone |

# 10 The Voyage

Preparations were in full swing and there was a lot of **hustle and bustle** aboard the ship all night, as the crew aimed to lift anchor by dawn. Jim felt exhausted by the end of it all and recalled that he had never in his life worked even half as much as that day. A little before dawn, the boatswain sounded his pipe and the crew began to man the capstan bars. Although weary, Jim was not ready to leave the deck and had no intention of missing a single moment of this new and exciting life. He enjoyed it all: "the brief commands, the shrill note of the whistle, the men bustling to their places in the glimmer of the ship's lanterns."

As the crew pulled up the anchor, John Silver led them into the familiar pirates' song:

> "Fifteen men on the dead man's chest—
>
> And then the whole crew bore chorus:—
>
> 'Yo-ho-ho, and a bottle of rum!"

As the sailors broke into their passionate **ditty**, Jim could not help but think of Captain Billy Bones. And soon *Hispaniola* left for its voyage into the land of treasure.

In the initial stages the hiccups seemed to be few: the ship was a good ship, the crew were capable seamen, and the captain thoroughly understood his business. So while there was not about the voyage to talk about, a few incidents needed mention.

One of the first ominous occurrences aboard the voyage was the disappearance of the first mate, Mr Arrow. A few days into the voyage and Arrow proved to be as useless as the fifth wheel. He was a worthless drunkard, who knew nothing about his job. He had no control over his men and moreover,was a bad influence on them. It was a mystery where he got his supply from and yet he was seldom **sober**. Arrow disappeared on a night of rough weather, apparently having fallen overboard in his drunkenness.It did not seem anyone regretted this loss.

After Arrow's disappearance, boatswain Job Anderson stepped up to this job. Although he retained his original title, he was serving as a **mate** too. The coxswain Israel Hands, a close companion to Silver, sometimes filled in too. Hands was an experienced seaman who could be "trusted at a pinch with almost anything."Squire Trelawney's knowledge of the sea made him very useful as well and the Squire sometimes took a watch himself.

Meanwhile, Jim continued to be **enthralled** by Silver, or Barbeque as his mates called him. It was amusing for Jim to see Silver's one-legged **maneuverings** across the deck: he could not help but admire his dexterity and thought that his smoothness of movement was comparable to any man who was in a perfect walking condition. Yet, some of Silver's mate, who all obeyed and respected him, expressed a great deal of pity to see Silver "so reduced", as they called it.

"He's no common man, Barbecue," the coxswain told Jim one day, describing Silver to be a well-learned and brave man, comparing his courage to that of a lion's.

"A lion's nothing alongside of Long John!"

Silver too was fond of Jim, always happy to see him in the **galley**, which he as clean as a new pin, the dishes hanging up burnished and his parrot in a cage in one corner. He would tell Jim stories about his 200-year-old parrot, Cap'n Flint, who happened to have sailed with notorious pirates. According to Silver, this parrot had seen more wickedness than anyone but the devil, and had learned to curse and scream from the **buccaneers** with whom she had travelled. Silver told Jim many interesting stories about past buccaneers and their voyages.

While friendship bloomed between Silver and Jim, Captain Smollett and Squire Trelawney still continued to be very distant. The Squire made no bones about his dislike for the Captain.

The Squire would say "A **trifle** more of that man and I shall explode."

The Captain on the other hand was a man of few words and spoke only when spoken to, giving sharp, staccato replies. He did accept when driven to the wall that he was somewhat wrong about the crew being **rogues**: he thought better of the men now and very highly of the ship.

The voyage continued and the ship was drawing closer to the destination. The island was expected to be in sight within the next 24 hours or less, and the end of the first part of the journey seemed near.

On that evening, Jim got hungry for an apple and walked down to the deck where the **barrel** of apple was always placed. There was one last apple left in the huge barrel and Jim had to bodily climb into it to get hold of it. The sound of the waters and the rocking movement of the ship caused Jim to almost fall asleep in the barrel and he was there a while. As he was trying to climb out, he was left shut in the barrel as a heavy man placed himself on its top. Hidden there, Jim accidentally overhears a conversation between Silver and another person, which revealed that things were not as they seemed.

### Glossary

- hustle bustle : a lot of activity, usually in a very noisy environment
- ditty : a short and simple song
- sober : to not be drunk
- mate : an officer on a ship
- enthralled : something that is interesting enough to attract your attention
- maneuverings : to cleverly plan something to get an advantage
- galley : the kitchen on a ship
- buccaneers : a pirate; originally a pirate of the Caribbean
- trifle : a thing that has very little importance or value
- rogues : people who are dishonest
- barrel : a container cylindrical in shape and made of wood

# 11 What I Heard in the Apple Barrel

Cloistered in the apple barrel Jim heard a conversation that was going to be a turning point for him and his mates. John Long Silver was conversing with the youngest sailor onboard, a mate called Dick. Jim learned that Silver was a **dreaded** pirate, as was most other men in the crew, whom Silver had so efficiently picked for Squire Trelawney. As he **recounted** the tale of his days under Captain Flint to young Dick, Jim overheard Silver say that he was indeed a friend of the blind beggar Pew. They both became **handicapped** on the same night, during a sea voyage under Flint: Silver lost a leg and Pew his eyesight. Most of Flint's men were now onboard the *Hispaniola*. Silver talked about the **pitiable** state many of his fellow pirates had got themselves into for not saving money in their heydays. Old Pew, lived like a king spending all he had, and was left with nothing at his retirement (due to blindness). Silver explained that he, though, was careful with his money. Unlike the rest of the "gentlemen of fortune" as he called the pirates,Silver had been saving money rather than throwing it away on rum and "a good fling." His goal, he revealed, was to "set up as a gentleman". While it could be impossible for Silver to set foot in Bristol after this voyage of **exploit**, Silver explained that his wife would empty his accounts his Bristol and join him in some secret place where they will both settle down.

Silver complimented Dick calling him smart and worth talking to frankly. Jim was seethed with rage to hear Silver use the same "words of flattery" for Dick that he had earlier showered on Jim. And like Jim, young Dick too was **engulfed** in Silver's charms and agreed to join him. At this point a third figure joined the two corrupt men and as soon as he spoke Jim recognized it to be the voice of Israel Hands.

The conversation continued to be **grimmer**, as more horrors were revealed. Hands seemed impatient and urged Silver to strike soon. He was unhappy that they had not mutinied yet against Captain Smollett and the rest of the men. However, the more calculative Silver advised against any such **haste**, and asked to wait until the time was right. Silver's plan was for the pirates to play their roles as honest seamen until the treasure was found and loaded. But he perceived that Hands and others may not have the patience for this, and urged them to bear with the Captain, Dr. Livesey, the Squireand the rest of the party of honest men for a few more days. Silver believed that they needed the Captain to **steer** the course for them until they reached the island, and later set a course for home. Although Silver and his men were all sailors, they did not know the location of the island, or where Dr. Livesey and the Squire hid the treasure map. Silver warned them to be patient or suffer the consequences, sighting the examples of Pew and Captain Flint, who both **perished** due to their impatience and **recklessness**.

The men also talked about what they intended to do with the "others" once the treasure was found. Silver seemed to have it all sorted out: he announced that the best option was to kill them as "dead men don't bite", and even claimed for himself the pleasure of killing Squire Trelawney.

"I'll wring his head off!"

Suddenly Silver asked Dick to fetch him an apple from the barrel sending a chill down Jim's spine for fear of discovery. However, Jim's luck held for then and he was saved, as the men quickly changed their mind and decided to drink instead. Silver instructed Dick to run up to where their secret keg was and bring them rum. It dawned upon Jim that this secret keg was where Mr Arrow was getting his alcohol from and Silver may have been behind his disappearance after all. While Dick was gone, Israel said to Silver that Dick would be last of the men to join them, suggesting that some of the crewmen had not sided with the pirates. As the men drank, the cry of "Land ho" was heard from the deck and they all rushed upstairs, leaving Jim an opportunity to make an escape,undetected.

A**myriad** of emotions overtook Jim: he felt angry, terrified, frustrated, and resentful, all at the same time.

## Glossary

| | | |
|---|---|---|
| ➢ dreaded | : | to fear greatly |
| ➢ recounted | : | to narrate in detail |
| ➢ handicapped | : | having a physical disability |
| ➢ pitiable | : | someone who makes others feel pity |
| ➢ exploit | : | utilize |
| ➢ engulfed | : | to cover or surround something |
| ➢ grimmer | : | dark and upsetting |
| ➢ haste | : | hurry |
| ➢ steer | : | to drive or operate a ship |
| ➢ perished | : | died |
| ➢ recklessness | : | being ignorant to dangers |
| ➢ keg | : | a small barrel |
| ➢ undetected | : | not noticed |
| ➢ myriad | : | a large number |
| ➢ resentful | : | feeling angry or annoyed |

# 12 Council of War

In the madness following the announcement of land, Jim slipped out of the barrel, reappeared on the deck, and managed to land beside Dr. Livesey and Hunter, as they all looked out for the sight of land. Gradually the fog lifted and there it was on the south-west side, two low hills separated by a couple of miles. Rising behind one of them was a third and higher hill, whose peak was still buried in the fog. All three seemed sharp and conical in figure.

Jim was in a daze, as if still reeling under the shock of what he had just heard. He tried hard to jerk himself back to senses, as he realized that the safety of his friends was now his responsibility.

The voice of Captain Smollett was heard: he ordered a course just to the east of the island. The Captain asked if anyone from the crew had been to this island before: Silver was **prompt** to respond and assured the Captain that there was a safe place to dock on the south side. Silver displayed sufficient knowledge about the geography of the island: the place was called the Skeleton Island, and it used to be a **den** of pirates. According to Silver the pirate called the hill on the north Foremast Hill. Of the three hills in sight, the one hidden behind the fog was the main one. Named Spy-glass by the pirates, as it served as a lookout, this was the spot where the pirates cleaned their ships.

At this point the Captain handed over a map to Silver, asking him to **corroborate** if the map showed the same place he was describing. Silver approached this task with bright eyes hoping that the chart being handed over to him be the treasure map; it was, however,an exact copy of the treasure map, with the treasure locations cleverly unmarked. Jim, now aware of the face behind the mask, was witness to Silver's quick change of expression from hope to **despair**. But Silver was too sharp in his game. He was fully his control of his emotions and not a soul doubted his **integrity** yet.

Jim begun to be frightened and guarded around Silver henceforth, but Silver continued to speak to Jim in the friendliest of ways, thus confirming he hadn't yet detected Jim's knowledge of their ominous **plotting**. Silver enthusiastically told Jim that the island was a great place to explore for a young lad like him, making known his own **fondness** for the place.

"You'll bathe, and you'll climb trees, and you'll hunt goats, you will; and you'll get aloft on them hills like a goat yourself."

Promising to pack a snack for Jim whenever he went exploring, Silver disappeared into the galleys. Jim was eager to bare it all to the older men. Finding the first opportunity he let Dr. Liveseyknow that there was some "terrible news" and requested a private **conference**along with Squire Trelawneyand Captain Smollett urgently. The doctor smartly communicated Jim's request to the others.

Captain Smollett called all men to gather on the deck and congratulated them on the first sighting of the island. The Captain announced to all hands that Squire Trelawney was very pleased with their performance and was going to send up grog (alcohol) for them. He led a cheer for the Squire, and another cheer followed for the Captain himself, this one led by Silver.

As the men got busy drinking, the three gentlemen retired to the Captain's cabin. Soon Jim was sent for, and it all seemed most ordinary. Once in front of the three men, Jim narrated everything he had heard without wasting a single minute. The men listened carefully without interrupting and almost without any movement.

Squire Trelawney immediately made a manly apology to the Captain, saying that the Captain had been right all along and theSquirewrong. He was now ready to await the Captain's orders. The Captain was quick to forgive the Squire, but apologized himself for not having **foreseen** the chances of a**rebellion** by the crew. However, they all agreed that Silver was a remarkable **mastermind** who not only had the entire crew in his firm control, but most convincingly charmed the Squire, the doctor, and Jim.

The Captain declared that they can't turn back now, because the men would rise against them. So they were going to keep sailing. The Captain believed they had time till the treasure was found, as the pirates would want to keep them safe until the destination was reached. Also, not all men were bad: there were a few honest crewmen, although it was almost impossible to separate the good from the bad. At that point if they had to make a list of men on their side, it would be SquireTrelawney's three servants, and the four of them.The doctor remarked that Jim could be very helpful in this situation. The men were willing to talk around him and Jim kept an eye open for everything. The Squire placed his trust on Jim too.

Jim felt anxious: they had counted only seven honest men against twenty-six men on whom they could not rely. And one among the seven, Jim, was merely a boy and supposed to be their **spy**!

## Glossary

- peak : the topmost part of a mountain
- daze : not being able to think clearly
- prompt : fast
- den : a sort of home
- corroborate : to show or agree that something is true
- despair : to lose all hope
- integrity : good or correct behaviour
- plotting : to make a secret plan
- fondness : to like or favour someone
- conference : meeting
- foreseen : to see or know about something that will happen in future
- rebellion : opposition or protest
- mastermind : someone who plans a difficult or complicated operation, especially a crime
- spy : someone whose job is to find out secret information

# PART III
# MY SHORE ADVENTURE

# 13 How my Shore Adventure Began

The next morning Jim walked up to the deck and got a clear look of the island. The ship had covered quite a distance overnight and was now lying calmly about half a mile to the south-east of the low eastern coast. Jim's excitement surrounding the adventure had now turned into **apathy**. Even the island looked unpromising to Jim and he hated it from the first sight.

Much of the island was covered in grey-coloured woods **interspersed** by yellow sand-breaks in the lower lands and large number of **mournful**-looking pine trees of varied sizes. The hills were all oddly shaped. Spy-glass was the tallest of all the hills by a few hundred feet and had by far the strangest **contours** – it had cliffs on all sides, while the top was flat like a table. The general look of the place was **gloomy** and grey. Meanwhile, the *Hispaniola* swayed side to side in the **swell**, making Jim seasick, and arousing an overall feeling of sickness.

It was going to be a long day. There was no wind, so the men had to get in boats and row, **hauling** the ship several miles up the island's eastern coast and into a narrow **strait** between it and the smaller skeleton Island, where the ship had to be anchored. Jim decided to help the crew sail and jumped into one of the boats, commanded by the boatswain Anderson. The crewmen were in a **surly** mood, screaming and hurling abuses at each other. On their return to the ship after a hot, sultry day, Dr. Livesey smelled **tropical** sickness in the air.

As noticed by Jim on the boat, by this point the crewmen had started showing signs of impatience and disobedience. They lay on the deck **grumbling**, and growling at the slightest orders.

Silver, however was on his best behaviour and in the best of spirits. Sometimes he tried so hard to please everyone that it seemed he was **compensating** for the crew's lack of manners. Moreover, Silver wanted to make sure that the Captain and his men were not **forewarned** of their plan by the crew's sudden change of **demeanour**. Silver was the person, who steered the ship to a safe landing on the south side of the island.

That evening Captain Smollett met with Squire Trelawney, Dr. Livesey, Jim, and the other good men. Squire Trelawney's servants Hunter, Joyce, and Redruth were taken into confidence. The Captain warned that the crew was in serious bad mood and if they had to hear any more from the Captain, they might soon break into war. The Captain believed that Silver could be of some help to them in this situation. Silver, unlike the others, was in full control of his senses, and would go any lengths to keep things smooth for the time being. The Captain suggested that the crewmen be given a day off that they may spend ashore, hoping that Silver would make the most of this opportunity to talk sense into his fellowmen. Meanwhile, the good guys were going to have a chance to **reclaim** the ship.

Thus decided, all seven men, including Jim, were given loaded pistols and the announcement of an afternoon ashore for the crew was made:

"My lads," said he (the Captain), "we've had a hot day and are all tired and out of sorts. A turn ashore'll hurt nobody – the boats are still in the water; you can take the gigs, and as many as please may go ashore for the afternoon. I'll fire a gun half an hour before sundown."

The crew was delighted to hear this and probably thought they would hit the treasure as soon they landed. Two boats were arranged by Silver, which were to take thirteen men ashore (including Silver). Six from the crew was left behind on the ship, along with the seven honest men.

Just as the boats were about to sail, Jim thought of a crazy idea; he realized that since six crew members were staying on, the Captain's plan of reclaiming the ship would have to be **stalled**. He thus decided to follow the crew ashore, and jumped into one of the boats, "curled up in the fore-sheets", purely on **impulse**. His efforts of slipping into the boat unseen, however failed, as Silver noticed him from the other boat and called out to him. No sooner had the boat sailed, Jim begun to regret his reckless decision, and yet what followed next was even more **venturesome**. As the boat reached the shore, Jim jumped out, quickly crawled to the beach, and scurried away into the island, ignoring Silver's calls behind him. He ran as far as he could and was soon out of sight of the group.

## Glossary

- apathy : lack of feeling or emotion
- interspersed : to insert at intervals among other things
- mournful : full of sorrow
- contours : an outline
- gloomy : feeling of sadness and hopelessness
- swell : grow or expand
- hauling : to cause to move by pulling
- strait : a narrow area of water that joins two larger areas of water
- surly : rude and unfriendly
- tropical : relating to an hot area
- grumbling : complaining
- compensating: to make up for
- forewarned : to alert someone about future dangers
- demeanour : the way one looks or behaves
- reclaim : to take back possession
- stalled : to come to a halt
- impulse : sudden strong feeling
- venturesome : risky

# 14 The First Blow

Jim **reveled** in his act of having given the slip to John Long and his fellow mates, and started to look around himself. Jim enjoyed his brief **solitude** and for the first time since the sighting of the islandfelt like exploring the place. At that moment, nothing stood between him and the **flora and fauna**of the unknown land,and he began noticing it with great interest. He had crossed the marshes, filled with willows, bulrushes, and other odd, **outlandish**, swampy trees; and landed on an **undulating** sandy terrain dotted with pines.Jim spotted flowers he had never seen and some snakes (Jim learned later one of these was a rattle snake), in this otherwise **uninhabited** land. One of the hills with two **craggy** peaks stood at the background.

As he explored further through the **thicket**Jim caught a glimpse of the Spy-glass. Suddenlythere was lot of bustle: the ducks were running all around, and birds were squeaking and circling the sky. Jim could feel the men approaching and heard the human voices. He crawled under the nearest live-oak and **squatted** there, **hearkening**, as silent as a mouse.

He heard two voices, one of which he recognized was Silver's. But from his position Jim could barely make out the words they were speaking. He felt a little desperate and reminded himself why he had risked sneaking into the pirates' boat and making way into the island. He crawled on all fours and began moving closer towards the two voices, until he could overhear as well as see them, while the men were completely clueless of this spy.

Silver was speaking to another crewman whose name, Jim learned from the conversation, was Tom. There seemed to be an argument going on between the two indicating that they disagreed with each other: Tom was against Silver's evil **enterprise**.Silver tried to **persuade** Tom to join the mutineers, but Tom stood firm for duty.For a moment Jim was relieved that he had found another on their side. However, this relief was going to be short-lived. Silver soon came down to threatening Tom while he refused politely to rise against the Captain.

At this point, a terrible noise, almost like a death-cry, was heard from a distance. Tom was **alarmed** but Silver was calm. Silver told Tom that that was the voice of another fellow called Alan, who had decided to stick to duty, just like Tom did. What they were hearing was Alan's last cries as he was being murdered by the mutineers on Silver's orders. Tom was, however, still **undeterred**. He turned his back on the **perfidious**Silver and walked away.

"If I die like a dog, I'll die in my dooty. You've killed Alan, have you? Kill me too, if you can. But I defies you."

But Silver would have his way. What Jim saw next was pure evil. Silver **clasped** the branch of a nearby tree for support and freeing his arms from the crutch he hurled it hard towards Tom. It hit him with great force, knocking him down. Then Silver walked up to Tom, "agile as a monkey even without leg or crutch", and stabbed him several times with his knife. That was the end of Tom. Jim was shocked to see this **monstrosity** unfold in front of him, and the world spanned above his head. After the slaying of the two righteous men, Alan and Tom, doubts about he himself being the next to be **slaughtered** upon discovery, lingered in Jim's mindand he was terrified out of his wits. Silver, however, was calm and unbothered. He cleaned his knife, picked up his crutch, and behaved like nothing unusual had happened. He brought out a whistle from his pocket and blew it, like a **holler** to the comrades.

Jim ran in frenzy. All he wanted was to escape these **gruesome** men and fled deeper into the woods without even looking to stop where he was going. Bleak thoughts about his future filled his mind: he instantly imagined that he will not be able to make it back to *Hispaniola* ever and would die on the island either due to starvation or in the hands of the pirates. He kept running until he had reached a hillier, more thickly forested part of the island. Then something made him stand stock still as his heart beat quickly.

## Glossary

- revelled : to celebrate or enjoy
- solitude : the state of being alone
- flora and fauna : plants and animals
- outlandish : from an outside country
- undulating : having a wavy surface
- uninhabited : not occupied or lived by people
- craggy : rough
- thicket : a dense growth of shrubs
- squatted : sit with one's knees bent
- hearkening : listening
- enterprise : operation
- persuade : convince
- alarmed : alerted
- undeterred : trying to do something despite setbacks
- perfidious : untrustworthy
- clasped : hold onto
- monstrosity : something evil or wrong
- slaughtered : murdered
- holler : call
- gruesome : causing horror
- bleak : not hopeful

# 15 The Man on the Island

In his flight from the pirates Jim had reached the side of a hill, where the ground was stony and steep. Suddenly he heard something **rattling** through the **gravel**. As he looked he saw a **shaggy** figure hiding behind the trees. Not only was Jim unsure about the **morphological** identity of this creature, he wondered whether this was a greater danger than the enemies he left behind.

The creature **flitted** through the trees like a deer, but Jim noticed it had two legs and hence it wasn't a deer. Little by little Jim recognized it to be a human, yet like no other human he had seen. Jim imagined he could be a **cannibal**.As he tried to weigh who was more dangerous, Silver or this creature in front of him, the very fact that he was human made him more approachable to Jim than the monster he knew Silver to be. Still **aghast**, he suddenly remembered he was not **defenceless** after all: there was loaded pistol on him! Courage started to resurface and he bravely walked up to this man.

As soon as Jim walking towards him, he took a step forward as well. He seemed confused: after a few moments of hesitation whether to walk up or flee away, he finally came forward, fell on his knees, and wrapped his **entreating** arms around Jim's waist. Jim was surely taken aback. The man introduced himself as "poor Ben Gunn" who had been living on this island for the past three years cut off from humanity.

"I'm poor Ben Gunn, I am; and I haven't spoke with a Christian these three years."

Finally assured that this person wasn't a threat, Jim **heeded** that he was a white man too and had a pleasing face. In terms of appearance he looked a sight; he was more **ragged** than any beggar Jim had seen or imagined. He had been roughed up by weather.

He was in tatters of an old ship's canvas and old sea-cloth, and this extraordinary patchwork was all held together by a network of things such as brass buttons, bits of stick, and loops of tarry gaskin. An old brass-buckled leather belt about his waist was the only solid in the whole **assemblage**. But his bright eyes stood out in a face darkened by extreme exposure.

He told Jim that he had been marooned three years ago. Jim knew "marooned" was a punishment among pirates, where they left behind the offender on a **desolate** and distant island, making it impossible to get back to land. Ben Gunn said he had been living on goats, berries, and oysters since then, surviving somehow. But he did crave a "Christian diet" and begged Jim for a piece of cheese. Jim promised him some cheese if he was ever to get back aboard the *Hispaniola*. Upon hearing about a ship, Ben Gunn's eyes shone. He seemed joyous to meet a fellow human and was extremely eager to exchange each other's stories with Jim.

He continued his **deranged** dialogues making many religious allusions and Jim almost believed he was crazy. He said he had a **pious** mother but nobody would know if they were to see him now. He told Jim that all this time alone on the island had turned him towards God and made him believe in Providence. He had even given up rum, except for "just a thimble-ful for luck, of course." Not only was Ben Gunn pious, he asserted that he was rich as well. He promised Jim that he would be good and share his wealth with Jim, if Jim helped him.

Hearing him talk thus, Jim was convinced now more than ever that Ben Gunn's solitude had made him lose his mind. Gunn scarily asked Jim if he had come to the island on Flint's ship. Jim told him that Flint was dead, but the ship that he had sailed on had some of Flint's men as crew, which was bad news for Jim and his mates. Jim was surprised when Gunn asked him if there was a one-legged man among them. Gunn asked Jim if he was on Silver's side, for if Jim was he would be of no help to Gunn. Jim began to realize that they may have a common enemy in Silver and narrated his own tale to Gunn without hesitation.

Gunn heard it all patiently and asked Jim to trust him. He told him that he was a crew aboard one of Flint's ships named *Walrus*.

One day Flint went ashore to bury the treasure accompanied by six other strong seamen. He returned to the ship alone, the others all murdered and buried by him. Then Flint commanded his mate Billy Bones and his quartermaster Long John Silver to sail away or be left ashore with the treasure, and so they did.Three years later Gunn was on another voyage and happened to spot the island during his trip. Gunn told his shipmates about Flint's treasure and the party came ashore to look for it. After spending twelve days and failing to find it, the frustrated sailors marooned Gunn with a **musket**, a spade, and a pick-axe; asking him to keep looking for the treasure.

Gunn promised to help out Jim and his friends (although Jim had no idea how), if in return he was given 1,000 British pounds and a safe passage home. He asked Jim to put in a good word for him to Squire Trelawney. Jim assured him that the Squire was a good man and would not refuse to take Gunn along in their ship; besides once the pirates are got rid off, men would be required on the ship to keep it sailing. Jim told him, but to make any of this possible he needed to go back to the ship himself and that seemed impossible to him. Gunn had a piece of good news for Jim: he showed him a boat which he had built in the past three years with the help of the tools he possessed. Jim and Gunn could sail back to the *Hispaniola* in that boat, hidden under a white rock.

Just then they heard a thunder of cannon fire and a "volley of small arms." Running towards the sound, they saw the British flag, the Union Jack, flying above the woods and realized that the fight had begun between the mutineers and the loyal men.

## Glossary

- rattling : making a kind of sound
- gravel : loose fragments of rock
- shaggy : someone with long, thick and uncombed hair
- morphological : relating to form or structure of things
- flitted : move swiftly
- cannibal : a person who eats the flesh of other human beings.

- defenceless : without defence or protection
- aghast : filled with horror
- entreating : to ask or beg for something
- heeded : paid attention to
- ragged : old and torn
- assemblage : a collection of things
- desolate : having no visitors or inhabitants
- deranged : insane or mentally unsound
- pious : being inclined to god
- musket : a shoulder gun

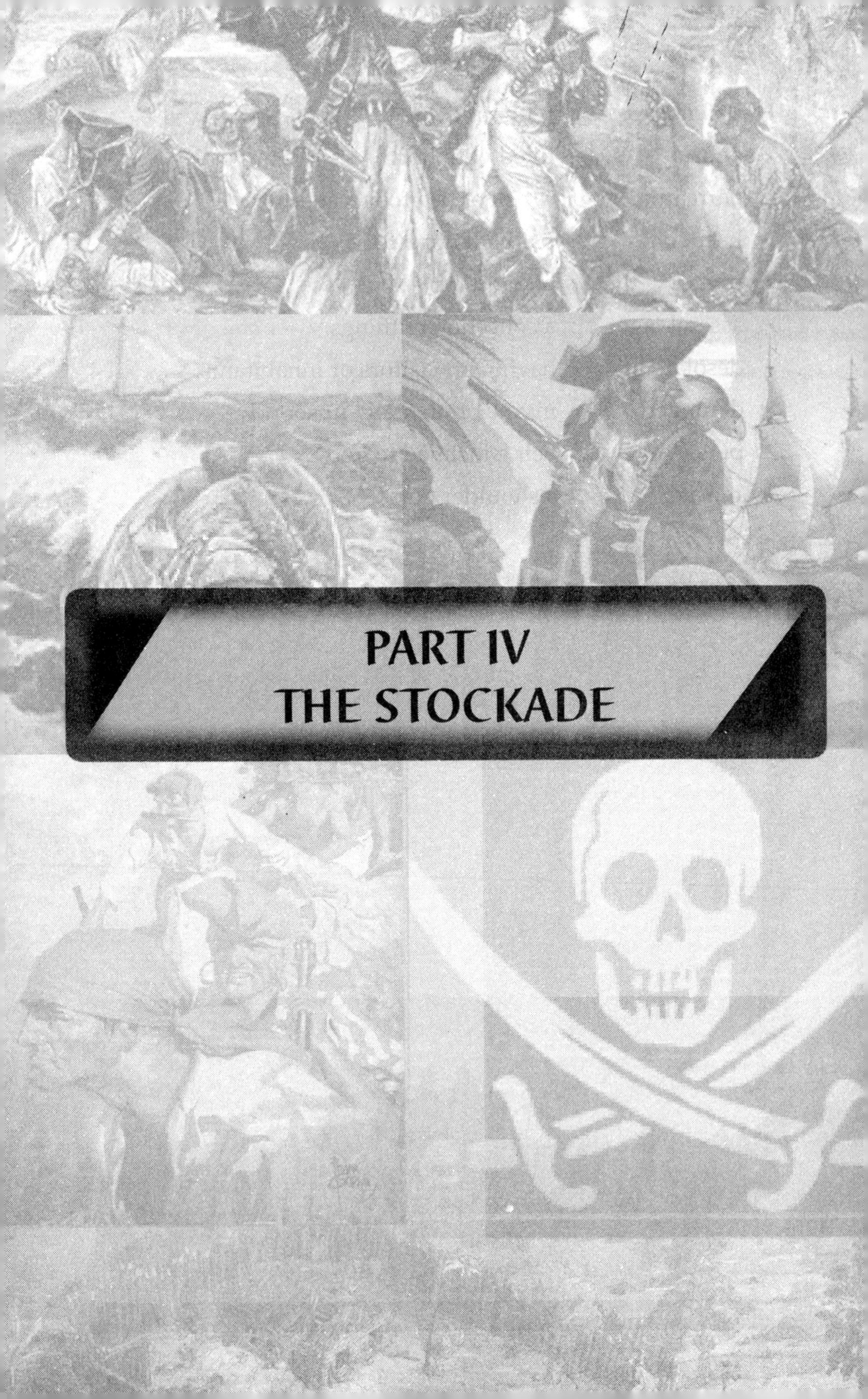

# PART IV
# THE STOCKADE

## 16 How the Ship Was Abandoned

We are once again taken back to the point in the **narrative** when Silver led two boats of soldiers ashore, with Jim hidden in one of them. Dr. Livesey, Squire Trelawney, and Captain Smollett were thinking how to **overpower** the mutineers left aboard and sail away. But the wind was not in their favour. Meanwhile, Hunter informed them Jim was not on the ship; thus putting all plans on hold.

Dr. Livesey knew the pirates who went ashore were in **foul** mood, ready to explode.The men were worried for Jim's safety. It was decided Dr. Livesey and Hunter would go ashore in a jolly-boat to find out Jim. As the doctor's boat approached the island, the two mutineers left to guard the shore party's boats caught sight of them. They were **ruffled** up a bit, but decided to stay where they were, and Dr. Livesey and Hunter steered around a bend, out of their sight. Upon landing on the island, the doctor found a stockade, the one he had seen on the map of the island.

Located on top of a hill, this was a large log house **equipped** with firing ports capable of holding about forty men, probably built by Flint and his men.A six-foot fence without any exit guarded this structure although there was considerable wide space all around between the fence and the house. The best thing was a spring of clear water flowed close by. Because this structure was near the top of a hill, Dr. Livesey understood that a small group of people could hold it against a much larger force **indefinitely** from there, if they had food and **ammunition** and kept a close watch to avoid any surprise.

What excited the doctor most was the source of clear water, for though the *Hispaniola* was stocked up with arms and ammunitions, variety of food, and excellent wine, they were running out of water. As he was thinking through the next course of action, he heard a loud shriek of a man. Not new to violent deaths, the doctor was sure what he heard was a death-cry and his heart sank as he thought of Jim.

Dr. Livesey made up his mind instantly, and with no time lost returned to the shore and jumped on board the jolly-boat. Hunter pulled a good oar and soon they were on the ship again. The men on the boat had heard the cries as well and they were shaken. Squire Trelawney, especially, had lost his colour blaming himself for having pulled the good men into this mess.

The doctor shared his plan with Captain Smollett: of them putting up at the abandoned stockade and defending themselves, and the two men worked on its **accomplishment**. Joyce and the doctor loaded the jolly-boat with powder tins, muskets, bags of biscuits, kegs of pork, a cask of cognac, and the doctor's invaluable medicine chest, to be carried to the stockade. The two men, accompanied by Hunter, made a second trip to the stockade. After a few rounds of to and fro between the boat and the stockade, the men managed to unload all supplies into the log house. Asking Joyce and Hunter to stand guard, the doctor rowed back to the *Hispaniola* with all his strength. The mutineers on guard seemed a little more alarmed on seeing the boat reappear.

On board the *Hispaniola,* Redruth was assigned the task of guarding the gallery between the cabin and the forecastle with loaded muskets and a mattress for his protection. The Captain and the Squireheld Israel Hands (the chief of the six mutineers on the ship) on gunpoint warning him against sending out a signal to Silver. Totally confused, but left with no option the six sailors went below the decks, surrounded by Squire Trelawney and Captain Smollett on one end of the ship and Redruth on the other. Upon the return of the doctor, the four good men began to load the rowboat for a second time with as much as it could hold, dropped the remaining guns and ammunitions overboard so the mutineers don't have access to it, and readied to abandon the ship. The Captain mentioned that he had noticed one of the mutineers, Abraham Gray, was not all bad, and could be persuaded easily to do his duty. The Captain gave a last call to Gray to leave the ship with the gentlemen's party. After a brief scuffle with the others, an injured Gray rushed out to the deck and declared his loyalty to the Captain. The good men jumped on to the boat and left the ship.

## Glossary

- narrative : story or account
- overpower : to overcome by force
- foul : offensive
- ruffled : troubled or bothered
- equipped : to be in possession of
- indefinitely : without any limits or end
- ammunition : explosives
- accomplishment : to succeed in making something happen

# 17 The Jolly-boat's Last Trip

Dr. Livesey's plan was working so far. But this final trip to the stockade brought its share of challenges. To start with the tiny boat they had all fit into was overloaded. Five grown men, of whom three - Trelawney, Redruth, and the Captain –were over six feet high, was already more than it was meant to carry. Add to that the powder, pork, and bread-bags. The boat listed to and fro with the weight. Terrified the men kept as still as possible.

Secondly, the tide had begun to **ebb** sending down strong currents. Dr. Livesey, who was steering the boat found it hard to manueuvre it towards the direction of the log house. The Captain and Redruth were on the oars, pulling as hard as they could. The Captain insisted Dr. Livesey continue **upstream**, or they will be lost in the sea. With great efforts the doctor battled the waves and steered ahead, so that although nearly **swamped** the boat was slowly making way.

Suddenly the Captain remembered the "Gun", a light nine-foot-long cast-iron gun that they had accidentally left on board the *Hispaniola*. Looking towards the ship the men saw Israel Hands and the four others were now in possession of the gun. The doctor remembered a round-shot and the powder for the gun had also been left behind, and it would be a simple matter for the **rogues** to get hold of those. To make matters worse, Gray mentioned Hands was Flint's gunner back in the day, which meant he was a great shot.

Meanwhile, the load and the tide had left the jolly-boat completely exposed and well within the range of the long nine. The good men saw and heard Hands preparing a shot on the deck. Among the men on the boat everyone agreed Squire Trelawney had the best shot, and the Captain asked him to pick up a gun and take down Hands. Hands **ducked** as the Squiref ired and the bullet hit one of the other mutineers who gave out a loud cry. This alarmed the group on the shore and a few of them jumped into one of the boats and started off for a **confrontation** with the people on the rowboat. The second pirates' boat was nowhere to be seen and the doctor's group realized that a batch of pirates must have rowed around to try and cut them off from the shore. Meanwhile, Hands was **unperturbed** by his injured comrade and continued to prepare the shot.

The Captain said to the party of the rowboat their aim would be to escape Hand's gunshot at any rate, and think about ways to deal with the pirates heading up to them later. By now they had made good progress for a boat so overloaded, and had drawn close to the beach; "thirty or forty strokes and we should beach her, for the ebb had already disclosed a narrow belt of sand below the clustering trees." Right then Hands fired his shot and as the men ducked to save themselves, the boat began to sink. They decided the safest thing to do would be to get off the boat and overturn it.The jolly boat sunk, taking down with it the supplies and three of their five pistols. The men **waded** to the beach unharmed.

Before they could hit the beach in their half-crippled states, they heard voices along the shore and feared the stockade might have been attacked.

## Glossary

- ebb : course or current of water
- upstream : in the opposite direction to the way a river or stream flows
- swamped : surrounded
- rogues : villains or hooligans
- ducked : to lower your head or head and body quickly, in order to move under something or to avoid being hit
- confrontation : to face your enemy directly
- unperturbed : not worried
- waded : to walk through water

# 18 End of the First Day's Fighting

The good men walked through a strip of wood to reach the stockade, and with every step they took the voice of the buccaneers became clearer and felt nearer. They prepared themselves for a confrontation with the pirates: Squire Trelawney was handed the Captain's gun as he was the best shooter in the group; Gray, who was unarmed was given Dr. Livesey's cutlass. Treading cautiously, the men could now see the stockade in front of them and were about to enter the enclosure. But unfortunately, at the very same moment seven mutineers with Job Anderson as the chief sprang into the enclosure, and both groups stood face to face. The mutineers were thrown for a few seconds, and before they even realized, the Squire, the doctor along with Hunter and Joyce from the log house had started firing at them. One of the mutineers fell dead and others ran to the trees for cover.

As the Captain's side **gleamed** in their small victory of causing the pirates to **flee**, pistol shots were heard from the bush, one of which hit old Tom Redruth. The Squire and doctor immediately returned a few shots at the bushes, but failed to get any of the mutineers down, although scaring them enough the disperse. The party turned their attention to the bleeding Redruth who had **collapsed** and carried him into the log house.

All was lost for Redruth, and the loyal, old servant accepted it without any complaint or fear. He had served the Squire well and followed every order silently; Squire Trelawney kneeled beside him and cried like a child asking his forgiveness for unknowingly dragging him to his death. Redruth forgave the Squire, asked for a prayer to be read as was the **custom**, and soon passed away.

Captain Smollett had been busy unpacking all the stuff he brought along stuffed in his coat: a couple of British flags, a Bible, a coil of rope, pen, ink, the ship's log, and lots of tobacco. When he noticed Redruth pass away, the Captain **reverentially** spread one of the British flags on his dead body, as the faithful servant had died on duty. The Captain was very busy setting up the house and counting the stores. With the help of Hunter, he set up the trunk of a felled, long fir tree at the corner of the log house, and from the roof of the house fixed the other British flag on it himself.

The Captain pulled the doctor aside and asked him how long they could expect someone to come for them. Doctor Livesey admitted that Squire's friend Blandly was to send a consort to look for them only if they did not return until after August. So it was possible that they might remain holed up in this fort for at least two months. Captain Smollett told the doctor they had plenty of arms but their food supplies were not going to last them long and since Redruth's death meant one less mouth to feed, it may be a good thing. He wanted to set up a party to salvage some of the things from the drowned boat, once the tide recedes; Gray and Hunter volunteered to step out at night when the forest is clear. However, before the Captain's men reached the boat, the mutineers had reached the spot and were seen carrying stores from the boat. They each had a loaded pistol in their hands.

Meanwhile, the firing from the *Hispaniola* continued. Squire Trelawney noticed since the house was invisible from the ship, the mutineers may be aiming at the flag that was fluttering outside. Captain Smollett, however, refused to lower the flag as it would not be "seamanly" to do so. Everyone agreed that the flag should stay and since the cannons were going overhead, they soon learned to ignore them.

Captain Smollet sat down to write a log of the day: he mentioned Redruth's death, the presence of the others, and just as he wondered what to write about Jim Hawkins, a voice is heard outside the house.

"Doctor!Squire! Captain! Hullo, Hunter, is that you?" came the cries.

## Glossary

- enclosure : an area surrounded by a fence or a wall
- gleamed : to smile in a certain way
- flee : to run away
- collapsed : to fall on the ground
- custom : something that people do that is traditional or usual
- reverentially : with respect
- salvage : to save

# 19 The Garrison in the Stockade

Jim was united with his friends. He learnt the British flag that had alarmed Jim and Ben Gunn earlier, was the same one **erected** in the stockade by Captain Smollett. The sighting of this flag was what brought Jim and the rest of party together.

As soon as Ben Gunn noticed the flag, he assured Jim of the presence of his friends somewhere around. He told Jim, the flag of England that was seen on the stockade, wasn't something the pirates would hoist; the mutineers had their own flag, called the Jolly Roger. Since they had heard shots being fired, a fight must have taken place between the two parties; and Ben supposed that Jim's friends must have "had the best of it". He told Jim about the stockade built by Flint, where he supposed Jim's friends had put up. Hearing as much, Jim couldn't wait to run to this place to the join Dr. Livesey and rest. But Ben wouldn't let him go until Jim promised to request the Squire and the doctor about Ben and his offer. He told Jim that he can find him back in the same place: but whoever came to meet him should bear a "white thing" in their hand, and come alone, between noon and six. Bentold Jim he had reasons of his own for this **proposal**.

Just about then, firing from the *Hispaniola* resumed, and Ben and Jim ran in different directions. Jim took cover in the woods as the cannonade continued; he went from one hiding place to another to save himself from the bullets. It was almost sun down when the **bombardment ceased**, and Jim **mustered** some courage to creep out of hideout and make way towards the stockade. He reached the shore-side from where he saw the *Hispaniola* with the Jolly Roger, the black flag of piracy, **upended** on the mast. He saw the men **demolishing** something with axes on the beach near the stockade, which he later learned was the jolly boat and how it happened to be there. After this short stoppage, Jim started to walk towards the stockade again. On his way he passed a white rock, and recollected Ben Gunn's claim that he hid a boat behind this rock.

With so many thoughts and sights in mind Jim finally reached the stockade and was relieved to find his friends there. Squire Trelawney, Dr. Livesey and the rest of the party warmly welcomed him and they quickly compared notes, bringing Jim up to speed on what had **transpired**. Jim looked about the log house; he found it to be an **unappealing** place and called it a "rude building". It was sandy - there was a "continual rain of fine sand. There was sand in our eyes, sand in our teeth, sand in our suppers, sand dancing in the spring at the bottom of the kettle"; and smokey - smoke "eddied about the house and kept us coughing and piping the eye". To add to the **distasteful**, was the depressing: Gray had a bandage tied around his face and the flag-draped corpse of Tom Redruth was still lying there.

As always, Captain Smollett decided to take matters into his hand and assigned duties to keep the blues away. He divided the group into two watch parties. Dr. Livesey, Gray, and Jim were in one group; and Squire Trelawney, Hunter, and Joyce were in the other. Two people were sent out to fetch firewood; two more were asked to dig a grave for Redruth; and the doctor was named cook. Jim was put on **sentry** duty at the door of the fort. The captain himself went from one to another, keeping up everyone's spirits and lending a hand wherever it was wanted.

The doctor kept having small conversations with Jim whenever he could steal a moment. Once he admitted to Jim that Captain Smollett was a great man, better than himself. Another time he spoke to Jim about Ben Gunn. Jim told the doctor Ben appeared slightly crazy, but the doctor thought a man in his condition can't be expected to seem entirely **sane**. He decided to take a piece of Parmesan cheese to Gunn soon, since that's what he wished for.

Before supper, Tom Redruth was buried in the sand. Later that evening, Doctor Livesey, Squire Trelawney, and Captain Smollett got together to discuss prospects and strategies for survival.The three gentlemen agreed that their best course of action would be to try and kill the pirates one by one, until they are so weakened that the survivors are forced to leave with the ship.Besides they had two more **accomplices**: rum and climate. Big drinker as they were, the rum would keep the mutineers dazed making them easy targets. Also the doctor believed that the climate and the camping near the swamp as it was would prove to be most unfavourable for the pirates, making them sick with fever soon. The pirates were heard singing drunkenly for long hours that very night, **validating** the doctor's **convictions**.

An exhausted Jim fell asleep while the conversations were still on. The next morning Jim woke up as he heard someone say "Flag of truce!" followed by the name Silver.

## Glossary

- erected : to build something
- proposal : a plan or suggestion
- bombardment : an attack on a place
- ceased : stopped
- mustered : to gather
- upended : to set
- demolishing : to break to pieces
- transpired : happened
- unappealing : unattractive
- distasteful : unpleasant
- sentry : a person standing guard
- sane : mentally fit
- accomplices : associates
- validating : to confirm as being true or valid
- convictions : beliefs

# 20 Silver's Embassy

It was a bitterly cold and damp morning, perhaps the coldest in their journey so far. Jim woke up in the stockade and **peeked** through a hole in the wall.In front of the **enclosure** stood Silver and one otherpirate who was holding a white flag.

Captain Smollett was **wary** of Silver's intentions and although Silver claimed he had come for **truce** talks, the captain was every bit suspicious of conspiracy. Asking everyone else to stay inside the log house and at watch, the Captain himself stepped out of the house to hear what the chief pirate, who was now being addressed as Captain Silver, had to say. Though Silver claimed that he was chosen captainby the "poor lads" after Captain Smollett deserted them,the Captain refused to acknowledge Silver's new name and rank. Silver asked the Captain to let him into the stockade, assuring the Captain that he had come to discuss terms that would be agreeable for both parties. Captain Smollett held his ground, and made it clear that he was least bit interested in what Silver had to propose. However, he **reluctantly** agreed to hear Silver out, warning him to be responsible for any **treacherous** attempts. Silver limped up the hill to the stockade and struggled a great deal to pull himself inside the fence, as the Captain watched **unfettered**. Silver hoped to be admitted inside the log house, at least to escape the harsh weather, but the Captain met Silver up front, not granting him the permission to walk inside the stockade or meet the others. The Captain reminded Silver; had he done his duty as an honest man, he would have been sitting in his own galley; but otherwise he was nothing but a common pirate who did not deserve any better.

It was not so easy to crush the cunning and calculating Silver.

**Unfazed** at this **inhospitality**,he placed himself on the sand. He peered and hurled **pleasantries** at Jim and Dr. Livesey. Captain Smollett was quick to remind him to finish what he had come for and get going. Silver said he had come to discuss an agreeable settlement for both parties, after the trouble of the previous night when the pirates, all drunk but Silver, were attacked and one was killed with a spike. He even mentioned that some of the shots fired the night before were good one, but it not such an attack to take place again. Now, Captain Smollett and the rest of the good men had no idea about this attack at this point: they were certainly not behind it and this was the first time they were hearing of it. However, the Captain wouldn't let Silver catch him confused. He played along, not letting Silver judge that the attack was someone else's doing.

Meanwhile, Jim was too overwhelmed with the happenings of that morning to stay put in his sentry duty, as ordered by the Captain. He had crept behind the Captain to give a good ear to the conversation between Silver and the Captain. On hearing about the attack, Jim was at first impressed with the **nonchalance** the Captain managed to show. But he soon remembered Ben Gunn's last words to him: Gunn had promised that were he to see the pirates camped ashore, there would be "widders (widows)" in the morning. Jim suspected that the attack might have been the work of Ben and he felt some relief to know that the number of their enemies were **diminishing** – "we had only fourteen enemies to deal with".

The Captain heard Silver patiently and waited for him to make an offer. Silver dived straight into the heart of the matter: they wanted the treasure. He said he was aware that the Captain and his people possessed a map of the island that could guide them to the treasure. He said if the Captain let him have the map, he will spare the lives of the Captain and his mates. The Captain refused the offer. Silver claimed he never meant any harm to any of them in the first place. On hearing such lies the Captain gave Silver a piece of his mind and the two men sat in silent for a brief moment, smoking their pipes.

Silver made a second attempt to convince the Captain. This time it was more than lives he was offering. He said if he was given the map and his men were not attacked again, he would allow the Captain and rest to come onboard the *Hispaniola* after the treasure is found and mounted on to the ship, and leave them somewhere safe ashore. Alternatively, Silver was ready to stock up the Captain's party with supplies from the ship, and the Captain and his men could stay on the island, while Silver arranged for another ship to come and pick them up. Silver mentioned that this was the handsomest offer the Captain would come across, and if the Captain refused it, it would mean the beginning of war between the two parties.

After hearing all, Captain Smollett put forth his own terms: if the pirates surrendered to him one by one, unarmed, he would chain them up onboard the ship and take them back to England for a fair trial. This was the good part of the offer. Otherwise, the pirates were doomed to die. They wouldn't know where to find the treasure, they did not know how to sail a ship, and they weren't even strong fighters: mostly drunk, even five of them couldn't keep Gray from escaping! The Captain said this was the last of them speaking, and promised to put "a bullet in your back" the next time he met Silver. The Captain **commanded** Silver to leave immediately.

Silver turned furious and **wrathful**. He **clambered** up with great difficulty, as the Captain watched him struggle, refusing to help him get up. Even though he roared for someone to help him up, no one from the house does. He swore that before an hour is up, the Captain and his men can expect an attack on their little fort. He crawled to the porch with great difficulty and limped his way down to the bottom of the hill where his **comrade** was waiting, and they disappeared behind the trees.

## Glossary

| | |
|---|---|
| ➢ peeked | to look secretly |
| ➢ wary | nervous about trusting |
| ➢ truce | an agreement |
| ➢ reluctantly | not willing to do something |
| ➢ treacherous | disloyal |
| ➢ unfettered | without limits or control |
| ➢ unfazed | not worried or upset |
| ➢ inhospitality | feeling not welcome |
| ➢ pleasantries | greetings |
| ➢ nonchalance | to show that one is not worried |
| ➢ diminishing | reducing |
| ➢ commanded | ordered |
| ➢ wrathful | strong anger |
| ➢ clambered | to climb awkwardly |
| ➢ comrade | associate |

# 21 The Attack

The Captain returned to the house after **dismissing** Silver and was **irked** to find all the housemates, except Gray, had left their sentry posts to witness the **parlay**. This was the first time Captain Smollett blew a fuse – "Quarters" he roared and everyone hurried back to their loopholes. The Captain did not forget to compliment Gray for sticking to his "duty like a seaman", and was especially disappointed with the senior men, Dr. Livesey and Squire Trelawney, for being negligent. The men were embarrassed to say the least; some proceeded to their loopholes, while others started loading muskets.

After a brief moment of silence, the Captain spoke again. He said they should be prepared for an attack in an hour's time. It was no secret that they were **outnumbered**, but they had the advantage of fighting from a protected enclosure. If they fought with discipline, Captain Smollett was confident they would win this uneven battle, and the Captain was just the man to lead them through this. He conducted a few rounds around the house to look into any loose ends that might have been left behind. He sounded orders for everyone telling them what to do and what to expect.

First and foremost, the Captain asked Jim to finish breakfast and be battle-ready. As the day had started to heat up, the fire in the house was doused to clear out the smoke. The Captain then began to set up his defence: Dr. Livesey was to take the door and fire through the porch; Hunter and Joyce were asked to guard the east and the west sides respectively. Squire Trelawney was the best shot in the group and was hence asked to take the most important position, the long north side with five loopholes. Gray was to accompany the Squire. The Captain decided, since he and Jim were not great shooters, they would be in charge of loading the muskets and would jump in whenever required. The men waited on pins and needles for an hour with no action happening. By then the day had become unbearably hot.

After a while, Joyce spotted the first pirate approaching and fired a bullet. And immediately the roar of the pirates was heard. Joyce's bullet was followed by a volley of shots from the other party, from all sides of the enclosure. Several bullets struck the log house, though none of them entered; Joyce returned a few shots, and then silence returned.The Captain decided to have a quick chat with this group taking an account of lost pirates, if any. They realized that the main attack was about to come and would come from the north side. When all of a sudden a bunch of pirates emerged from north side of woods, and made it straight towards the stockade. The firing from the pirates had **resumed** alongside, as one of bullets sailed through the doorway and shattered the doctor's musket to pieces. The pirates began to climb over the fence, while the Squire and Gray continued to fire openly at them. There were seven who were trying to enter the stockade. In the exchange of fire two were killed, while one ran for life; four others, however, managed to land inside the stockade to lead a direct attack. Meanwhile, the other mutineers kept up the firing, although **futile**, as the bullets only managed to hit the walls of the log house.

Headed by boatswain Job Anderson, the four mutineers who had set foot within the stockade led a direct and fierce attack. Suddenly, it was the mutineers who seemed to be on top of things. They ran towards the house: one of the pirates pulled at the **nozzle** of Hunter's gun that was poking through one of the loopholes, and knocked out Hunter with it. Another appeared at the doorway and attacked the doctor with a **cutlass**. Two others swarmed inside the house and confusion **ensued**. The Captain ordered everyone to bring out the cutlasses for a close fight, as the guns were only disadvantaging them. Soon everyone was fighting in the yard. Instantly, Jim grabbed a knife and jumped into the middle of the **combat**. He received a cut across his knuckles and without waiting to stop who his attacker was, he ran out of the house.

Running about the house with a cutlass raised in his hand, Jim was suddenly face-to-face with the cutlass-bearing Anderson. To escape Anderson's blow, Jim **leaped** to his side and was sent rolling down the slope headlong. By the time Jim found his foot again, the tables had turned yet again. Gray, who was following close behind Jim, had slain Anderson and two other had been struck down as well. Meanwhile, Dr. Livesey pursued his assaulter down the hill and managed to stab him. Only one out of the four who had climbed into the stockade was alive then, and Jim watched this pirate clamber down and flee in mortal fear. Later, the doctor, Gray, and Jim raced back into the stockade, fearing **retaliation** from the survivors.

For the moment, victory was on their side. But it was not without a price. In the house, Joyce lay dead, shot through the head; the Captain and Hunter had been wounded as well. The group mulled over their situation: the odds were in their favour. While theirs' was a four-man army now, the death of five pirates in that day's fight meant the Captain's team had only nine more mutineers to defeat.It is only much later the good men learn that the pirate Squire Trelawney had shot from the jolly boat had died too, leaving them eight enemies.

## Glossary

- dismissing : rejecting
- irked : be angry
- parley : conversation
- outnumbered : be fewer in number to comparison to the opposition
- resumed : continued
- futile : useless
- nozzle : the front part of a gun
- ensued : to take place
- cutlass : a short, curvy sword
- combat : a fight
- leaped : jumped
- retaliation : to strike back at an enemy

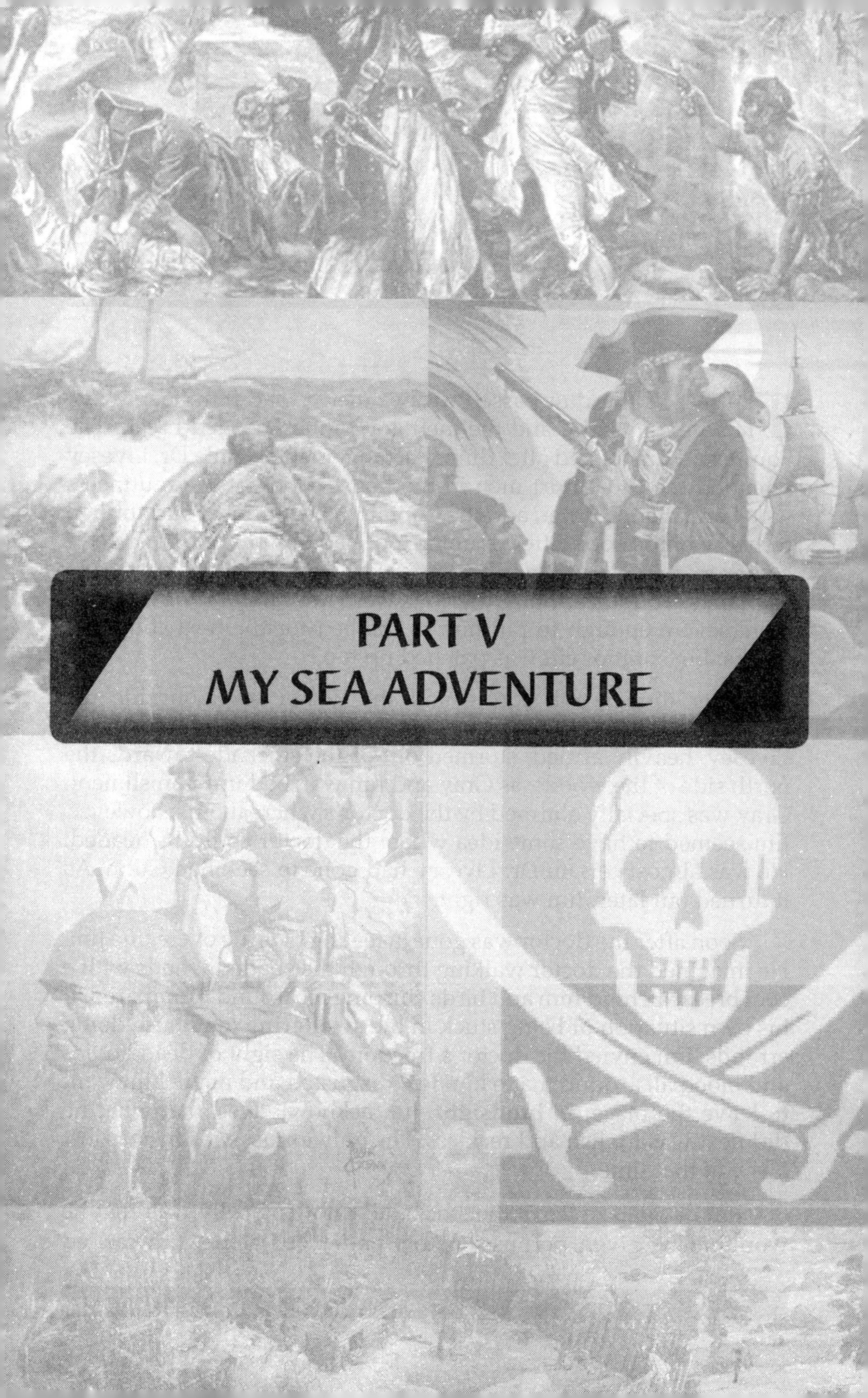

# PART V
# MY SEA ADVENTURE

22

# How My Sea Adventure Began

The rest of the day passed away quietly. The mutineers were nowhere in sight, and the men got a much-needed break. The Squire and Jim looked after dinner arrangements, while Dr. Livesey attended the three hurt men in the house - one of the mutineers who had fallen, Hunter, and the Captain. The mutineer **succumbed** to his wounds soon after. Hunter too, had slipped into a state of coma from grave wounds and passed away the night after. The Captain's wounds although serious were not **fatal**. However, they were severe enough to pin him to the bed for the next couple of weeks. Jim's minor cut was patched up too.

After dinner, the Squire and the doctor sat alongside the Captain to discuss the state of things. After they were done, Dr. Livesey, heavily armed, stormed out of the stockade towards the north side of the woods, as Gray and Jim watched in astonishment. Gray was specially alarmed by the doctor's whereabouts; however, Jim seemed to have some idea where the doctor could be headed. He was almost certain Dr. Livesey had gone to seek Ben Gunn. As it turned out later, Jim was right.

Soon after the doctor was gone, a feeling of **envy** overcame Jim. He imagined the doctor walking through the shaded woods with a cool breeze behind him and birds chirping all around. Compared to his own situation of being stuck in the **sweltering** log house doing errands, Jim envied the doctor's freedom. The sight of dead bodies and blood all around made him feel disgusted and made him want to leave the place. In **hindsight**, Jim acknowledged that what he did next was foolish and reckless. His only excuse was he was just a boy at that time.

Jim decided to leave the stockade. Knowing fully well that he wouldn't be given permission to wander out alone, Jim carried out his plan on the sly. He filled his pockets with biscuits and a brace of pistols, and as soon as an opportunity presented itself, he gave everyone a slip (the Square and Gray were busy helping the Captain dress his wounds).

As foolish as his act seemed at that time, it was discovered later that had it not been for Jim, the Captain and the others would have died at the hands of the pirates. With the enemy close at hand, there was no doubt that it was risky to leave the stockade at the care of only two men in fighting condition. Jim admitted, "This was my second **folly**, far worse than the first, as I left but two sound men to guard the house; but like the first, it was a help towards saving all of us."

Jim, however, did not just want to stroll down the woods; he had a plan. He decided to walk down to the sandy pit that separated the anchorage from the open sea, reach the white rock he came across while making his way to the stockade the first time, and ascertain if the boat Ben Gunn had spoken about was actually lying there. After slipping out of the house, Jim headed for the east coast of the island and finally reached the sea. He began to stroll beside the surf and enjoyed the sea breeze for a while. He kept walking cautiously avoiding the anchorage and the pirates' camp, until he was in front of the sea from where he could see the *Hispaniola.* The Jolly Roger, the black flag of the pirates, was fluttering on its mast. The Spy-glass stood tall behind.

Beside the boat Jim spotted a small boat and there were three men laughing and talking around it. Jim recognized Silver at once, with two of his other comrades. Suddenly a loud, scary voice startled Jim, reminding him of Captain Flint. He saw Silver's parrot Cap'n Flint **perched** on his wrist. A little while later, the two comrades hopped onto the rowboat and sailed off in the direction of the ship. Just about the same time, the sun went down behind the Spy-glass, and darkness began to descend. Jim reminded himself that he must lose no time if he had to find Ben Gunn's boat that evening. From where he stood, the white rock was visible to him, but it took a while to **tread** the path to it, sometimes crawling on all fours through the brush so as not to be seen.Almost at nightfall, he reached the rock and was relieved to find a very tiny boat made of wood and goat-skin parked there: this was Ben Gunn's boat. The boat seemed so small that Jim imagined even just one full-sized man would fit into it with some difficulty.

"The thing was extremely small, even for me, and I can hardly imagine that it could have floated with a full-sized man. There was one thwart set as low as possible, a kind of stretcher in the bows, and a double paddle for propulsion."

It reminded Jim of the **coracle** boats of ancient Britain, and he described the boat as the worst version of the coracle he had seen. But on the brighter side, it was light and **portable**. While his initial goal was to find the boat, Jim had a new plan in mind, albeit even riskier than the first venture of stepping out of the stockade. With the boat in front of him, Jim decided to row out quietly to the *Hispaniola* under the cover of the night, cut the rope attached to the anchor, and let the ship **drift** shoreward.

This would prevent the pirates from escaping to sea after their defeat. Jim waited for full darkness and had a meal of the biscuits he had brought along. Finally, when all is black, he groped his way out of the hollow near the white rock and caught sight of two points of light: one of them was the fire the pirates had lit on the shore around which they were drinking and **carousing**; the other light was coming from the ship, where Jim was headed.

## Glossary

- succumbed : to be taken down by something
- fatal : causing death
- envy : jealousy
- sweltering : extremely hot
- hindsight : the chance to judge past events
- folly : mistake
- perched : sit on something
- tread : walk
- coracle : a small boat used in Britain from ancient times and made of a frame (as of wicker) covered usually with hide or tarpaulin
- portable : easily movable
- drift : driven along by wind
- carousing : odrinkalcoholandenjoyyourselfinanoisyway

# 23 The Ebb-tide Runs

Jim began his journey to the ship. The coracle, as Jim called it, was hard to steer. While the coracle managed to remain **buoyant** and was a clever piece of work, because of its lightness and littleness, it was best at turning round and round, no matter how much Jim tried to keep it straight. Even Ben Gunn himself had admitted that it was "queer to handle till you knew her way."

For some time Jim struggled: the boat turned in every direction except the one Jim wanted it to, until luckily the tide turned in Jim's favour and the current pushed his tiny boat towards the ocean as the *Hispaniola* rose in front of him. The next moment the **hawser** with which the ship was bound lay next to Jim, so close that he could get hold of it. Jim grabbed the hawser and felt some tightness as the tide was pulling the ship upon its anchor. He readied to cut off the ropes with his sea-**gully** hoping to send the ship humming down the tide. But it occurred to Jim that if he cut the rope all at once while it was pulled tight, it would snap back and pull both him and his boat out of the water. He waited a while thinking, when fortunately the wind turned in his favour pulling the *Hispaniola* into the current, **slackening** the tight hawser still in Jim's grasp. Jim took out his gully and started separating the ropes from the ship, one strand at a time, till the huge vessel was swung by only two. He decided to hold off cutting the last two strands till the wind lightened the strain on the hawser a little more and pointed the ship in the opposite direction of him and his boat.

During his brief pause, Jim's focus was drawn to the voices coming from the cabin. He recognized one of the voices to be of Israel Hands. There was another pirate with Hands; the two men were drunk and angry, and yelled rude oaths at each other. On the shore behind him, Jim could see a great camp-fire burning; one of the sailors was heard singing a **morbid** sea-song, a ship setting out with a crew of seventy-five and returning with only one alive.

*"But one man of her crew alive,*
*What put to sea with seventy-five."*

Jim felt the song suited the happenings of that morning; the cruel losses that were suffered. At last there was a breeze and Jim was about to cut the last few ropes attached to the ship, when suddenly on a whim Jim yet again undertook a risky business. Curiosity got the better of him and he clutched on to one of the trailing ropes and hauled himself to the window level of the ship and peered through the cabin window. By this time the ship had started gliding swiftly through the water and had almost fetched level with the camp-fire. But the pirates on board had not raised an alarm and Jim tried to comprehend why there was no **apprising** yet. Through the cabin window he saw Hands and the other pirate wrestling with each other in a state of massive drunkenness: luckily for Jim, between their **inebriation** and fight the pirates did not realize that they were now in motion.

Jim landed himself back on the coracle with a sharp jump. The pirates on the shore had now broken into the familiar sailor's song:

*"Fifteen men on the dead man's chest –*
*Yo ho-ho, and a bottle of rum!*
*Drink and the devil had done for the rest –*
*Yo-ho-ho, and a bottle of rum!"*

Suddenly the coracle lurched to the side. Ripples started to gather all around the little boat. The *Hispaniola* herself tilted slightly and began wheeling southward: towards the open sea instead of the shore. The ship turned with such a jerk that even the pirates noticed it this time. Jim, whose boat was being carried in the wake of the *Hispaniola,* feared the worst from this change of course: he worried that he and his little boat will be swept out to the open sea. Jim helplessly lied down at the bottom of his boat, almost trying to hide, and certain that he would soon run **aground** on rocks and die. However, the constant rocking of the boat made him grow so exhausted that he fell asleep in the boat while waiting for his impending death; he dreamt of his old life back at the Admiral Benbow Inn.

## Glossary

| | | |
|---|---|---|
| ➢ buoyant | : | capable of floating |
| ➢ hawser | : | a heavy cable or rope that is used for tying up or pulling a ship |
| ➢ gully | : | a large knife |
| ➢ slackening | : | slowing up |
| ➢ morbid | : | relating to death and disease |
| ➢ apprising | : | to tell someone about something |
| ➢ inebriation | : | state of being drunk |
| ➢ aground | : | if a ship runs aground, it becomes stuck on a piece of ground under the water, where the water is not deep enough |

# 24 The Cruise of the Coracle

It was broad day when Jim awoke and found himself tossing at the south-west end of the Treasure Island. The sun was hidden behind the great bulk of the Spy-glass. The two other hills - Haulbowline Head and Mizzen-mast were in front of Jim too; this edge of the island bound with cliffs forty or fifty feet high and fringed with great masses of fallen rock. Jim's first instinct upon waking up was to paddle to the shore, but he soon realized the shortcomings of this venture.If he was to come close to the shore he would either be dashed by the rocks, or have a difficult time attempting to climb the cliffs, ultimately failing. Moreover, he noticed a bunch of huge, slimy monster-like creatures crawling on the shore and dropping into the sea with loud noises.

"...two or three score of them together, making the rocks to echo with their barkings."

These creatures made hitting the southward shore off limits for Jim:"I felt willing rather to starve at sea than to confront such perils." He later learnt that they were harmless sea-lions.

He instead decided to row the coracle northward. He remembered what Silver had told him about the northward current and seeing that he was already under its influence, Jim decided to steer towards the less threatening coastline and reach the Cape of the Woods, an areaburied in tall green pines. For a while, Jim had a smooth sail - the boat carried him easily along the current. He was surprised at the ease and dexterity with which the little boat could ride. But hereafter Jim decided to do something bold, almost **jeopardizing** his secure spot. He tried to row in a different position and paddle the boat: every time he paddled the boat rocked violently almost **capsizing** a few times.

Quick to realize his folly, Jim instantly fell back to his originally position and lay quietly in the boat on his elbows, only giving one weak stroke every once in a while to keep the bow pointed towards shore. The coracle surely had a mind of its own which was not to be interfered with; as soon as Jim let go it started sailing softly as before.

Slow and tiring though, Jim was gradually able to guide the coracle close to the shore. He reached a point where he could see the green tree-tops swaying in the breeze and was almost certain of making a landing. Jim started to feel sick overcome by thirst and fatigue; his throat was **parched** and his head was aching, making him desperate to land soon. Just around the bend then he saw the *Hispaniola* about half a mile away and the landing plans came to a halt. Jim realized that he would be found and captured, but he was so thirsty that he almost didn't care.

The ship was sailing, headed northward. Jim thought that it was being taken back to anchorage, but suddenly noticed that it wasn't sailing anymore. Then again it would start moving backward and forward, almost directionless. Jim assumed there could be two possibilities: either the pirates were steering the ship in a state of drunkenness or they had abandoned the ship, which meant it wasn't being steered at all. At this point, yet another bright idea crossed Jim's mind. He began to believe that if he could get himself aboard the ship he would be able to retake control of the vessel until Captain Smollett wasbackin control.

Jim used all his strength to paddle his rowboat towards the ship: the two vessels moving towards each other, the ship way slower than the coracle. As Jim drew closer, the ship stood still making it a little more difficult for him to reach her. Then suddenly with the shift of the current, the *Hispaniola* turned sharply and started moving towards the rowboat with great speed, bow first. Jim was in a dangerous situation as the rapidly moving ship was about to collide with the coracle any moment now. Left with no option, Jim leaped to his feet, caught the bowsprit of the ship (the part of the spar reaching beyond the ship), and hung from it, the coracle sinking below him. Hewas hanging on to the ship for dear life, but at the same time he realized that there was no way of escaping from the ship.

## Glossary

- shortcomings : a fault or problem that makes someone or something less
- jeopardizing : putting oneself or others in danger
- capsizing : if a boat capsizes, it turns upside down or onto its side in the water
- parched : extremely thirsty

# 25 I Strike the Jolly Roger

Jim was scarcely balancing himself on the bowsprit when the flying jib flapped and almost hit him, nearly throwing him into the sea. He swiftly crawled up to bowsprit and landed himself on the front deck of the ship. At first glance the vessel seemed deserted. The planks, which had not been **swabbed** since the mutiny, bore the print of many feet, and an empty bottle, broken by the neck, tumbled to and fro like a live thing in the **scuppers**. Then suddenly the ship heaved to the side swinging the mainsail up in the air: Jim got a view of the after-deck and there was Israel Hands and the other pirate,**sprawled** on the floor like dead bodies.

Hands was propped against the bulwarks, lying with his arms stretched out and his face had lost colour. The other pirate too was lying with his arms stretched out and his teeth showing through his open lips. As the ship swayed, his body was **lurched** to and fro, and he did not seem to move a muscle in spite of this roll and roll that he was being subjected to. Of the two men, he was certainly dead. The pools of blood that had **accumulated** all around made Jim wonder whether Hands was dead too: he assumed the two must have killed each other. All of a sudden then, Israel Hands turned and moaned in pain. Jim walked up to the mast where the men were lying and greeted Hands ironically: "Come aboard, Mr. Hands".Pain and weakness had taken over Hands so much, that he was barely surprised to see Jim and he could say was "Brandy".

Jim realized that Hands was in a delicate situation and any delay might cause him to pass out again. He rushed down to the cabin to look for brandy. It was a scene of utter chaos down in the cabin: all the locks had been broken to look for the treasure map, the floors were thick with mud from the **ruffians** walking around after wading in the marshes round their camp, and dozens of empty bottles clinked together in corners to the rolling of the ship. One of

Dr. Livesey's medical books lay open on the table, half of the leaves gutted out, Jim assumed for pipelights.

In the cellar all the barrels were gone, as were most of the rum bottles. He found one, however, as well as grabbing some biscuit, fruits, raisins, and cheese for himself he went back up on the deck. He sat down in front of Hands and began to eat as Hands gulped down the brandy. Hands was sort of **revived** after the dose of brandy, and he began to speak. He told Jim that had Dr. Livesey been around, his wounds would have healed with some assistance from the doctor, but unfortunately he did not have that kind of luck. Jim told Hands that he had come to take possession of the ship, and Hands must consider him captain until further notice. After he was done eating, in a symbolic gesture Jim cut off the pirate's black flag –the Jolly Roger – and threw it overboard, as Hands watched this show of power.

"And there's an end to Captain Silver!"

Although Hands was not very **keen**, he was left with no option but to do as Jim said, and help him sail the ship. He pointed to his dead mate (O'Brien as we later learn his name was) saying he was of no help in sea-business. Addressing Jim as Captain Hawkins, Hands said he imagined that Jim wanted to get to shore. He made a deal: if Jim was to give him food, drink, and a scarf to tie his wound, he would help Jim navigate and sail the ship. Jim commanded that he would like to sail towards the North Inlet, rather than the anchorage where the pirates had camped. Hands agreed and they struck the **bargain**. He offered Hands one of his mother's silk handkerchiefs, which he scoured out of his own chest and helped Israel Hands wrap up the stab wound on his thigh. After some more brandy, Israel Hands was perked up and sat up straighter.

Jim felt pleased with himself for what he had accomplished. He was delighted that the weather and wind were now favourable, and was fascinated by the new views of the coast. He no longer felt as guilty for having crept out of the stockade in secrecy: he believed his friends would forgive him when they learn that he had conquered the ship. However, the way Hands kept looking at him made him uncomfortable. It was as if Hands was keeping an eye on him, his eyes full of treachery.

## Glossary

| | | |
|---|---|---|
| ➢ swabbed | : | to wash a floor, especially with a mop |
| ➢ scuppers | : | to spoil someone's plans or hopes of success |
| ➢ sprawled | : | lying or sitting with your arms and legs stretched out in different directions |
| ➢ lurched | : | to move suddenly in a way that is not smooth or controlled |
| ➢ accumulated | : | to collect up over a period of time |
| ➢ ruffians | : | villains |
| ➢ revived | : | make conscious again |
| ➢ keen | : | interested |
| ➢ bargain | : | deal |

# 26 Israel Hands

Jim and Israel Hands managed to steer the *Hispaniola* to the northern end of the island. They were about to approach the Northern inlet when the wind turned, and since they had no anchor, they waited for the tide to turn to beach safely. The ship was brought to a halt, and Jim and Hands sat, resting and eating in silence.

Finally Hands broke the silence. He diverted Jim's attention to the dead body of O'Brien lying on the deck and started convincing Jim about having it disposed of the ship. Jim wasn't in favour of this: he declined the proposal saying he wasn't strong enough for the job. Hands raised the pitch about the *Hispaniola* being an unlucky vessel which had seen great many deaths, and the lying around of a useless **corpse** on the deck would only bring more bad luck. But Jim was **obstinate** too, he told Hands that the body may have passed, but the spirit of O'Brien might be watching them.

"You can kill the body, Mr. Hands, but not the spirit; you must know that already," Jim replied. "O'Brien there is in another world, and may be watching us."

After this futile discussion, and some more talk about the nature of death, Hands asked Jim to fetch him some wine, as the brandy was too strong and was messing with his head. Jim had by now guessed what Hands' real intentions were: through the proposal of disposing the dead body and now the request for the wine, Hands was trying to get Jim off the deck, so that he could have the place unobserved for a while. However, what he would do in this time was yet unclear to Jim.

"He wanted me to leave the deck – so much was plain; but with what purpose I could in no way imagine."

Jim decided to grab this opportunity to find out what Hands was up to. He was sure that if he could hide his suspicions and played along, he will be able to get the better off Hands. He readily agreed to go and look for some wine in the cabin. He ran below making a lot of noise to convince Hands that he was actually getting wine. As soon as he was down, he slipped off his shoes and ran quietly along the empty gallery to take a position from where he would be able to see Hands, but the latter won't know. Jim took every precaution possible to stay hidden and watch Hands. Unfortunately, the worst of his suspicions proved true.

Hands wasn't as wounded as he pretended; he could very well move. Jim saw him moving about the deck. He crawled through the deck to reach the port scuppers, pulled out a bloodstained knife out of a coil of rope, and quickly hid it in the **bosom** of his jacket. He limped back to his original position and sat exactly like Jim had left him, trying to give the impression that he hadn't moved at all.

Jim now knew that Israel Hands could move and he was armed. He felt sure that Hands was going to kill him. Although, he did believe that Hands wanted to take the ship ashore as much as he did, and so until the *Hispaniola* was sheltered in a safe place, Jim would probably stay unharmed. He gathered his thoughts, then grabbed a bottle of wine, and walked back up to the deck. On seeing Jim, Hands continued his **pretence** of ill-health. He knocked off the neck of the wine bottle and took a good swig raising his favourite toast: "Here's luck!" He asked Jim to cut a quid of tobacco for him as he had no knife. Angered by his lies and treachery, Jim almost rebuked Hands, saying that a man like Hands should spend his time in prayers as he had betrayed the crew, killed men, and had lived sinfully. Hands, however, maintained a calm solemnity and in his defence said to Jim that in his 30 years as a seaman he had never seen anything good happen to a good man.

In a while, the tide was favourable and it was about another two miles to the shore. But the navigation had to be delicate, as the entrance to this northern anchorage was not only narrow and **shoal**, but lay east and west, so that the vessel had to be nicely handled to be got in. Jim felt he was doing a decent job at steering the ship, following closely Hands' instructions, as was an excellent pilot. The certainty and neatness with which they made way, Jim **reckoned** would be a pleasure to see. Hands pointed out a beach to

Jim for docking the ship. Jim was trying hard to maneuverthe ship and got so thoroughly involved in the running of the vessel that he almost forgot about the **lurking** danger (Israel Hands) behind him. Suddenly he turned – may be purely on instinct or may be heard a creak or saw his shadow with the tail of his eyes – and there was Hands approaching him with a knife in his right hand.

Cries were heard from both sides: Jim's was a shrill cry of fear, but Hands almost gave out a roar of fury and **pounced** upon Jim. Jim leapt to the side letting go of the steering lever, which hit Hands on the chest. This blow left Hands breathless for a few moments, giving Jim the time to reach out for one of the pistols. By the time Jim aimed at him, Hands was once again coming at him; he drew the trigger but nothing happened as the sea-water had foulled the pistol. Jim cursed himself for not having **prepped** himself a little in advance, since he knew this was coming.

Hands was coming towards Jim with exceptional speed for an injured person. Jim realized that the worst thing would be to run inside the ship: that way he would be cornered and Hands would easily overpower him. Instead he stood there, preparing to **dodge** the knife whenever the blow came. Seeing Jim's move, Hands stopped too; he showed a few moves and Jim responded correspondingly. It reminded him of the games he used to play at Black Hill Cove, though never with his heart beating so hard.

Then all of a sudden the *Hispaniola* ran aground into the sand and the deck tilted by about 45 degrees. Both the men were sent down rolling into the scuppers, the dead body of O'Brien following behind them. Jim was the first to be on his feet again, while Hands was trying to free himself from the clutches of the dead body with which he had got entangled. Having the advantage of being quicker than his enemy, Jim quickly climbed the ropes to the **mizzen mast**,rattled up hand over hand, and did not draw a breath till he was seated on the top. He lost no time in reloading two pistols, certain of firing from at least one. Hands was in a spot, the climb was going to be **daunting** for him. But left with no option, he began to mount, taking up an enormous amount of time and letting out plentiful **groans** to bear the dragging of his painful leg behind him. Jim threatened to fire his limping enemy if he kept climbing.

"One more step, Mr. Hands," said Jim, "and I'll blow your brains out!"

Hands, however, seemed to reflect that he was in a bad position, and he offered to come to an agreement with Jim; but, even as he was speaking, he threw the knife suddenly, pinning Jim by the flesh of his shoulder to the mast. In an act of defence, Jim fired both pistols and dropped them, almost unconsciously, and Hands fell into the water, head first. That was the end of Israel Hands.

### Glossary

- corpse : dead body
- obstinate : being stubborn
- bosom : chest
- pretense : to show something that is not true
- shoal : a group of fish that swim together
- reckoned : believed or understood
- lurking : to wait, sometimes hiding, in order to frighten, annoy, or attack someone
- pounced : to quickly jump on or hold someone or something
- prepared : to prepare for
- dodge : to avoid something by moving quickly
- mizzen mast : the mast aft or next aft of the main mast in a ship
- daunting : challenging
- groans : to make a long low sound when one is in pain

# 27 Pieces of Eight

Seated **atop** the mast, Jim watched the sea below him. Hands' body was lying close by in the water; it bobbed up to the surface once and then sunk, not to reappear again. As the water settled, Jim could see him lying on the clean, bright sand in the shadow of the ship's sides. A fish or two whipped past his body. Jim was now certain that he was dead and ironically laid as food for fish in the very place where he had designed Jim's slaughter.

Jim himself started feeling sick and terrified in his high position. The knife wound **inflicted** by Hands was bleeding causing him some pain. However, it was not so much the physical discomfort that made him feel faint: he wanted to get off the mast as quickly as possible as he feared that he might slip and fall into the green water next to Israel Hands' body.

He clung on to the mast with great force and shut his eyes until he regained his **composure**. He tried to pull the knife out from the part of his skin it had pierced, but it seemed stuck. As he pulled at it, he **shuddered** with pain. Oddly enough, it was this shuddering that somehow freed him from the knife, which had mostly pinned his clothing and the farthest edge of skin. He eased out of his shirt, and lowered himself to the deck. He did what he could to care for his wound: although it bled and pained for some time, it wasn't anything severe and Jim could still use his arm to the best of his ability. Next, Jim decided to get rid of O'Brien's dead body and claim the ship entirely. Jim took him by the waist as if he had been a sack of bran and with one good **heave**, tumbled him overboard. The pirate on the ship thus went in the water with a **plunge**.

Jim was alone on the ship. The tide had turned and the sun was about to set. As the wind rose, Jim tried his best to bring down the sails so that the ship would not be damaged by being blown about. He cut the halyards (ropes) so that part of the main sail was no longer underwater: loose canvas floated down to lie across the surface, but Jim couldn't tug down the rope to move the mast anymore, so he left it, trusting the *Hispaniola* to luck. He jumped into waist-deep water and started wading ashore.

Jim was pretty pleased with himself for what he had achieved. As he left the water to reach the shore and began his journey towards the stockade, he imagined that even the righteous Captain Smollett would forgive his escapade when he learns that Jim had reclaimed the ship. He looked forward to meet his friends in the log house. The sun had set by then, making it difficult for Jim to track the path. He crossed a stream along the woods and came close to the spot where he had met Ben Gunn. He saw a fire around that place and assumed the man of the island Ben was cooking himself supper. However, it did strike Jim that it was unusual for Ben Gunn to be this careless: a fire such as this would be easily visible to the pirates and thus draw a lot of unwanted attention.

Gradually it turned darker, and Jim found it harder to find his way. Until suddenly there was a gleam of silvery brightness that took over: the moon was shining brightly and climbing higher and higher in the sky. In the advantage of the sudden **luminance**, Jim rapidly treaded the rest of the journey to his destination, sometimes walking, sometimes running. Finally, he reached the borders of the clearing: there were signs of a bonfire that had just burned out. Other than that it was dark and silent all around. Suspecting that something might have gone wrong, Jim started crawling to reach the stockade. He was relieved to be greeted by snoring noises, which he assumed was coming from his friends. While he was glad to be back, he felt concerned that no one kept a watch: if he could **sneak in** so easily, so would Silver's men. As he tried to make way in, he stumbled upon a person's leg in the dark, who groaned but did not wake. And then, all of a sudden, a shrill voice broke forth out of the darkness:

"Pieces of eight! Pieces of eight! Pieces of eight! Pieces of eight! Pieces of eight!"

It was Silver's parrot and it went on without pause or change. Jim realized that the stockade was now under the possession of the pirates. But there was no time to run. The parrot successfully woke up the sleepers, who grabbed and captured Jim, as Silver's voice is heard asking one of his men to **fetch** a torch.

## Glossary

- atop : at the top of something
- inflicted : to cause something unpleasant to happen
- composure : the feeling of being calm, confident, and relaxed
- shuddered : sudden shaking of the body due to fright or pain
- heave : to push, pull, or lift a heavy object using a lot of effort
- plunge : to fall quickly from a high position
- luminance : glowing light
- sneak in : to enter secretly
- fetch : to bring

# PART VI
# CAPTAIN SILVER

# 28 In the Enemy's Camp

In the light of the torch Jim saw the clearer picture. The stockade and its supplies had been captured by the mutineers: there was a cask of cognac, there were pork and bread, but there were no sign of any prisoner. Jim feared the worst.He guessed that his friends might have been killed and felt miserable for not having been there with them.

There were six mutineers in the house apart from Silver: five of them seemed unharmed as they had risen to their feet stunned by Jim's entry, while the sixth one was wounded and lay there looking. Silver stood in front of Jim, his parrot, Cap'n Flint, perched on his shoulder. He looked paler and sterner than before. He said that it was a pleasure to have Jim Hawkins back and seated himself across the room and began to fill a pipe. Silver remarked that Jim appeared smart to him initially, however his **truancy** was beyond Silver's understanding. Jim kept up a bold outward appearance, although he realized all was lost, especially with his friends gone.

Silver began to speak. He told Jim that he had always been fond of him and still was. Meanwhile, Captain Smollett and Doctor Liveseydid not have the best opinion about Jim in light of recent events concerning him. The Captain wouldn't forgive Jim for **dereliction** of duty and the doctor too thought what he had done was ungrateful and almost traitor-like. Silver said that his friends wouldn't be willing to take Jim back in their fold, and Jim was left with no option but to stick with Silver. Jim was more relieved than distressed to hear what he heard: he was happy that his friends were alive. Silver asked Jim what he thought of the proposal, though he said Jim could take his time and no one would hurry him. Jim understood that Silver wanted him to choose between death and joining the pirates. Jim felt **infuriated** inside and started to answer boldly. He demanded to know what had happened to Captain Smollett and the others.

Silver told him that one morning Dr. Livesey had come to him bearing the flag of truce. He brought the news that the ship was gone and there was nothing left for both parties. A bargain was struck and the pirates were given the stores, brandy, the possession of the log house, and firewood. Dr. Livesey and the rest had left, and Silver did not know where they were presently. Silver pointed out that the doctor had formally **denounced** Jim as not being one among them during the bargain. His last words to Silver were: "As for that boy, I don't know where he is, confound him… We're about sick of him."

However, Jim refused to make a conscious choice and gave an **emboldened** speech to the mutineers baring it all. He said he was not afraid of anything any longer and hardly cared about his own life. He revealed that it was him who had hid in the apple barrel and heard Silver's council with Hands and Dick. He was the one who first got to know of the mutineers' evil design and apprised his friends. It was Jim who had set the *Hispaniola* free and later captured it, killing the pirates on board and taking the ship into hiding. He concluded by saying simply that if he was **spared**, he would try his best to save the pirates in court as a **witness**. He also said, if the pirates were to kill him, he would like Silver to inform Dr. Livesey of that.

The pirates stood staring at Jim as he spoke. They were **flabbergasted** to know that young Jim was responsible for all that was happening. One of them, Morgan, suddenly remembered that it was Jim that had given away Black Dog back at the Admiral Benbow Inn; Silver **pitched in** saying it was Jim that had stolen Billy Bones' treasure map as well. Having understood that Jim thwarted them at every step, Morgan drew out his knife, ready to launch an attack on Jim. The other pirates were with Morgan in this. However, Silver **forbade** the mutineers from harming Jim. He ordered the lot of them to step back and dared them to disobey him as they seemed unwavering. Silver vouched for Jim to be one of the best boys he had seen and almost forced the pirates to back off and submit to his authority. After a long silence, one of the men said that although Silver was the elected Captain among them, the crew was dissatisfied and upset with such bullying from Silver. They asked for a council outside without Silver, pointing out they had a right to this kind of meeting by the rules of piracy. One by one each man slipped out, leaving just Silver and Jim.

Silver grabbed this opportunity to strike a deal with Jim, agreeing first and foremost that the game was very much up. Silver told Jim that the pirates were unhappy with him and were going to **overthrow** him by mutinying against him. Meanwhile, Jim's chances of surviving were next to none. Silver promised to protect Jim from the pirates, if Jim agreed to bear witness for him when he is taken to the court of law. Silver said he was now on the Squire's side. Jim agreed to try his best for Silver, however, he wondered how that was going to be possible since Silver had been the **ringleader** of the whole disaster. He promised to not betray Jim and his friends again, as he was aware that all was lost in this side. Moreover, it would be foolish of him to upset Jim since he was the only one who knew where the ship was. In the end Silver asked Jim whether he knew why Dr. Livesey had handed over the treasure map to Silver. Jim was shocked to learn this; from his expression Silver learnt that Jim had no idea why the doctor had done that.

## Glossary

- truancy : the act of disappearing from somewhere without permission
- dereliction : intentional or conscious neglect
- infuriated : very angry
- denounced : to criticise someone or something severely in public
- emboldened : confident and bold
- spared : saved
- witness : someone who sees a crime, accident, or other event happen
- flabbergasted : shocked
- pitched in : to join other people in doing a job
- forbade : to tell someone that they must not do something
- overthrow : to force a leader out of their position of power
- ringleader : leader of a group who does something wrong

# 29 The Black Spot Again

Jim and Silver waited in the house as the pirates held their **council**outside. One of the pirates returned for a moment to borrow the torch from the house and immediately joined the group again, leaving Jim and Silver in the dark. Jim **peered** through one of the loopholes and saw a kneeling figure with a book and knife in his hand. One of the pirates was holding the light for the one on his knees, while the others all watched. Then they all marched back towards the house.

Quite hesitantly then, one of the pirates handed over something to Silver: the black spot. Silver did not seem surprised or scared; only, he was **appalled** to see that the pirates had **ripped** a page off the Bible to use as paper. Silver questioned that who had the **audacity** to commit this awful act and upon learning that it was Dick Johnson who cut the circle of paper out of the Bible, John Silver assured him that he was doomed. George Merry, one of the other pirates asked Silver to focus on attention on the words written on the other side of the paper. They had written "**deposed**", the **unanimous** decision of the pirates to not have Silver as their Captain any longer. Silver acted with great calmness and reminded the crew that rules lay down that before being removed from official duties of a Captain, Silver should get a chance to clarify himself. He requested that the crew voice their **grievances** and let him answer them, before they proceed. George Merry listed out all the complaints: Long John Silver had messed up the whole plan; he let their enemies leave their fort just because they wanted to; he prevented the pirates from attacking their enemies as they were leaving the fort; and he let Jim Hawkins live.The pirates felt that they were all going to hang because of Silver's mistakes.

Silver replied to each of their grievances one by one. Firstly, he pointed out that Anderson, Hands and George Merry were the pirates who had made mischief and had messed up the affairs from the start. It was they who decided to mutiny before the treasure was found. Secondly, Silver had bargained with the Squire's group to gain the supplies in the stockade and, more importantly, the treasure map; thirdly, the reason he did not allow that group to be followed and killed was so that the doctor could visit the wounded men and Merry himself, who was sick with fever; and, finally, Silver was against killing Jim because they could be used as a **hostage** to make a deal. Saying all he had to, Silver let the pirates have the treasure map. With this unexpected surprise, the pirates began to see sense in all what Silver said and reason in what he had done. They grabbed the map with utmost delight and curiosity and started **analyzing** it by passing it from hand to hand. However, George Merry wondered how they could use the map without a ship. Silver reminded them that it was Merry's men who lost the ship due to their **foolhardiness**. Meanwhile, Silver was the one who gained the treasure map for them. He rested his case with this final statement, asking the mutineers to decide who the better man was. The group once again sided with Silver and cried that they wanted him as their Captain, rather than George Merry.

All settled between the pirates, Silver handed over the black spot to Jim to satisfy his curiosity. Jim examined it closely: one side contains a verse from Revelations, including "Without are dogs and murderers," while on the other side has been scrawled, "Depposed." Jim kept it as a memento.

At night Jim laid awake in bed **pondering** upon Silver's cleverness and **tact**. He managed to make the pirates happy, while desperately trying to save his own life. Jim thought it was dangerous game that Silver was playing. Inspite of all the wickedness Silver had shown, Jim couldn't help but feel sorry for him – the shameful gibbet (**gallows**) that awaited him.

## Glossary

- council : a group meeting
- peered : to look carefully
- appalled : offended or shocked very much by something
- ripped : torn off
- audacity : courage
- deposed : to force a leader out of their position of power
- unanimous : agreed by all
- grievances : complaints
- hostage : a person who is the prisoner of someone who threatens to kill them if they do not get what they want
- analyzing : to study or examine
- foolhardiness : ignoring obvious dangers in a stupid way
- pondering : thinking over
- tact : a careful way of speaking or behaving that avoids upsetting other people
- gallows : a wooden frame used for killing criminals by hanging them from it with a rope around their neck

# 30 On Parole

The next morning Jim is woken up by Dr. Livesey's voice, as he came visiting to the stockade. Although Jim was glad to hear the sound, yet his gladness was not without **admixture**. A feeling of embarrassment and shamefulness engulfed him as he thought of his recent conduct of abandoning the doctor and the rest. Jim looked at him through a loophole, ashamed to face him.

Silver greeted Dr. Livesey cheerfully telling him that his patients were doing well. He also told the doctor about the re-appearance of a little stranger. Dr. Livesey was quite shocked to learn that Jim was back. He took a moment to gather himself and without speaking to Jim, proceeded to see his patients first. The doctor carried on with his business of tending the injured pirates with so much calm that it seemed that he was paying an ordinary professional visit in a quiet English family. The pirates too behaved as if nothing had occurred– as if he was still the ship's doctor and they were still a bunch of faithful crew.

Dr. Livesey assured the mutineers that he would do his best to keep them alive for the trial and subsequent hanging back in England. After finishing his medical duties, he requested to let him have a word with Jim. Immediately the pirates arose in protest. George Merry was the first to say a firm No. Silver **intervened** and silenced the mutineers. However, he asked Jim to swear that he would not go against the deal they had made and run away. Jim readily promised to do as agreed.

Silver asked Dr. Livesey to step outside the stockade and wait for him to bring Jim along. As soon as the doctor was out of sight, the pirates attacked Silver for agreeing to let the doctor meet Jim. They accused him of playing double–of only looking to save himself, and sacrificing the interests of his accomplices and victims, and, in one word, of the identical, exact thing that Silver was doing.

Surprisingly for Jim, Silver yet again managed to defend himself handily, and promised the pirates that he would kill the doctor himself as soon as he was no longer needed.

Silver then **escorted** Jim across the sand to where the doctor was waiting for them. Silver decided to make his case first to the doctor. He told him that Jim would **testify** how Silver had saved Jim's life and in doing jeopardized his position to such an extent that he was handed the black spot by his fellowmen. He hoped that Dr. Livesey would take this into consideration when judging Silver. The doctor asked him if he was scared of punishment; Silver replied he wasn't a coward, but he would do his best to avoid being hanged. So saying, Silver stepped back a little way, till he was out of earshot, and there sat down upon a tree-stump and began to whistle. He kept a watch on both sides: sometimes he looked at Jim and the doctor and sometimes his **unruly** crewmen.

Doctor Livesey greeted Jim sadly and told him that he was disappointed that Jim ran off like a coward the minute Captain Smollett got injured. The doctor told Jim that he would face as he deserved. Jim was already ashamed of his conduct and began to cry upon finally facing Dr. Livesey. He said he knew he was doomed.

The doctor's heart melted on seeing Jim blaming himself and he suggested that they run way. Jim was not ready to break his promise to Silver. However, he admitted that he was scared of being tortured. He feared that he would succumb and reveal where the ship was. At this point Jim told the doctor that it was he who had let the ship sail and had docked it at some place away from the sight of the pirates. He told the doctor the location of ship.

The doctor was surprised to learn this and Jim explained to him the sequence of events that transpired since he left the stockade. Doctor Livesey felt a sort of pride upon hearing Jim's adventure. He promised that he would save his life and **acknowledged** the fact that it was Jim who had saved their lives more than once: first by uncovering the plot and then by finding Ben Gunn.

The doctor then called out to Silver and told him to keep away from the treasure as much as possible. But Silver admitted that it might be difficult. The only way to save his and Jim's life may actually be taking the pirates to the treasure.

Long John Silver asked why Doctor Livesey gave him the map in the first place. But, Doctor Livesey disagreed to share anymore at that point. The doctor promised to do his best to save Silver if they both survived. He advised Silver to keep Jim close by his side and to watch out for **squalls**. With that, Doctor Livesey headed back into the forest.

**Glossary**

- admixture : mixture
- intervened : to become involved in a situation in order to try to stop or change it
- escorted : to go somewhere with a person in order to protect them or to prevent them from escaping
- testify : to make a statement about something that you saw, know, or experienced, usually in a court of law
- unruly : very difficult to control
- conduct : behaviour
- acknowledged : to accept or admit
- squalls : a storm that happens suddenly, especially at sea

# 31 The Treasure Hunt —Flint's Pointer

As soon as they were alone again, Silver acknowledged his gratefulness to Jim for not agreeing to run away with Dr. Livesey. He had been keeping an eye on the doctor and Jim as they spoke, and was glad that Jim decided to keep the promise he had made to Silver. With this **gesture** of Jim, Silver was now hopeful of saving his own life. The pirates were about to launch the treasure hunt and Silver advised Jim that they should stick to each other as much as possible.

One of the men called out to them that breakfast was ready and they all ate together. Jim was appalled to see the amount of food the pirates were wasting, although knowing fully well that supplies were limited.

Thus he kept running on, with his mouth full of the hot bacon; thus he restored their hope and confidence, and, I more than suspect, repaired his own at the same time. Silver seemed least bothered about this recklessness and started giving the pirates false hopes by saying that they will soon find the treasure. He leads them on by saying that since they had the boats to carry treasure to the ship, they had the upper hand in the game. Although they were yet to learn where the ship was, he assured them that they will be able to locate the ship too once the treasure was found. Silver also reminded the mutineers about Jim's usefulness as a hostage. He said that they could use Jim to get back the ship, and sail off in the ship with the treasure.

The naïve pirates were cheered up by these false promises, but Jim wondered if Silver would actually do what he said if they found the treasure. Silver's cunningness made Jim suspicious of his actual intentions: he had a foot in either camps, and there was no doubt that he would prefer wealth and freedom than a bare escape from hanging, which was the best he could hope if he sided with the honest men. Jim further thought even if Silver decided to keep his faith with Dr. Livesey, what would happen if his followers found out the truth. Silver and Jim against five strong and active seamenwould be an ill-matched contest.

Add to this, Jim felt completely **clueless** about why his friends deserted the stockade and given away the treasure map. Harder still to understand was the doctor's last warning to Silver, "Look out for squalls when you find it".

With all these thoughts in his mind Jim set forth behind his**captors** on the **quest** for treasure.

A cord was strung around Jim's waist and he was led outside the log-house by Silver who was armed with guns and a cutlass, his parrot perched on his shoulder. The others carried the **provisions** with them, and marched slowly to the beach. On the way, the pirates discussed the chart: the red crosses were large enough to be confusing, and the directions were somewhat **ambiguous**. The chart mentioned a tall tree, Spy-glass shoulder, the direction E.S.E. and Skeleton Island. As they walked each person pointed to a different tall tree as being the one, but Silver ordered them to continue straight ahead anyway.

The party continued to follow the directions laid out on the map. They first landed at the mouth of the second river shown on the map and from there began to **ascend** the slope towards the plateau. It was a beautiful area filled with heavy-scented broom and many flowering shrubs. Thickets of green nutmeg-trees were dotted here and there with the red columns and the broad shadow of the pines.

They had walked for about half a mile and were approaching the plateau when one of the men was heard shouting and the other proceeded in his direction wondering if the treasure had been found. However, what awaited them at the sight was something very different. At the foot of a pretty big pine lay a human skeleton on the ground with some clothing on it.

After a few minutes of scare, George Merry walked up near the skeleton to examine it. Looking at its clothes, he remarked that he must have been a seaman. As everyone observed it more carefully, it seemed impossible that the body was in a natural position. The man laid perfectly straight—his feet pointed in one direction, his hands, raised above his head like a diver's, pointed directly in the opposite.

Soon Silver figured out that it was not merely a skeleton. It was a direction that was left behind by the twisted Flint (one of the six men he killed). The compass and the body pointed in the same direction.

The pirates even recognized the dead person as a sailor called Allardcye. They began to talk about the frightful Flint, his wickedness and bad temper, and the men he had killed. They were all visibly freaked out on **stumbling upon** the dead sailor's remains. One of the pirates claimed to hear Flint's sailor song. Silver chided him, saying Flint was dead and it can't be his voice. He urged them to keep going, but the pirates continued to remain frightened.

## Glossary

- gesture : a movement that communicates a feeling or instruction
- clueless : knowing nothing
- captors : someone who is keeping you as a prisoner
- quest : a long and difficult search
- provisions : things that will be required
- ambiguous : not clear
- ascend : to climb a mountain
- stumbling upon : to fall or almost fall while you are walking or running

# 32 The Treasure Hunt—The Voice Among the Trees

The party climbed a hill and then stopped to rest: partly alarmed by a **recap** of Flint's horrific nature and partly to rest Silver and the sick folk.

Before them was a vista of much of the island. They could see the Skeleton Island and the sea on the east. There was no sound anywhere but that of the distant breakers, mounting from all round, and the chirp of countless insects in the brush. The emptiness of the island underlined the sense of solitude.

Silver fidgeted with his compass while resting and **cheerily** remarked that they should be pretty close to the treasure. Morgan told him that recollecting Flint has had a bad influence on him and he did not feel so well. The other pirates agreed, although Silver reminded them that he was dead.

Ever since they had found the skeleton, the pirates had spoken lower and lower, and they had almost got to whispering by now. Then all of a sudden, out of the middle of the trees, a thin, high, trembling voice was heard, singing the familiar sailor song:

"Fifteen men on the dead man's chest—Yo-ho-ho, and a bottle of rum!"

The pirates were struck by horror it seemed. They all went pale and Merry muttered **disbelievingly**, it was Flint! The song had stopped as suddenly as it had began. Silver, too seemed a bit shaken at first, but he quickly brushed it off. He assured the pirates that the voice cannot be of a dead man and someone was fooling around with them. The pirates were beginning to see some sense in what Silver claimed, when yet again the voice was heard. This time it uttered "Fetch aft the rum, Darby!", which Morgan whispered were the final words of Flint. The pirates were yet again overcome by fear and they voice still in dread. Dick had taken out his Bible and had begun praying.

Silver, although **rattled** had not yet accepted that it was the dead Flint's voice. He did agree that nobody other than the pirates knew of Flint's last words, and so it may be possible that they were hearing Flint. But he was not ready to give up on the mission and told the mutineers that he was not afraid of Flint when he was alive and so he will face his ghost as well to acquire the treasure, which they were now so close to. But the pirates had lost all courage and were not eager to carry on.

Silver presented one last argument to awaken their courage: he said that the voice echoed, and that was proved it was a human voice, rather than a spirit. Just like spirits don't have shadows, they can't produce echoes, Silver reasoned. This argument was convincing enough for George Merry and Morgan, and they seemed to suddenly believe that the voice sounded like someone else's.

Suddenly Silver shouted that it sounded just like Ben Gunn's voice. But Dick said that it doesn't help, since Ben Gunn could not have been on the island either. However, Merry and the other older pirates are of the opinion that if it was in fact Ben Gunn there was nothing to be afraid of, since nobody was scared of Gunn, whether dead or alive.

Their spirits of the pirates had returned and the natural colour had revived in their faces. Soon they were chatting together, andhearing no further sound, they shouldered the tools and set forth again.Dick was the only one among them who was still frightened and had begun to fallill as well.

The group **marched** across the plateau and attempted to dig under several trees in their path, as each turned up nothing. Finally they approached a huge, 200-foot tree, and the pirates' eyes burned with excitement, their feet grew speedier and lighter, and they started dreaming about a future of **extravagance** and pleasure that they thoughtwas waiting there for each of them.

Silver seemed half mad with excitement at this sight. From time to time,he turned his eyes upon Jimto give him a **menacing** look. As the treasure seemed within reach, Jim realized that all else had been forgotten: Silver's promise and the doctor's warning to him were both things of the past.

The pirates began to speed up, so much so that Jim stumbled a few times, only to be pulled roughly at the rope by Silver. Jim's head is filled with negative thoughts: he felt alarmed about Silver's upcoming betrayal, and was also troubled to imagine that the plateau they just passed had once been a site of six murders by the cruel Flint. To see Dick getting sicker and sicker only added to Jim's woes.

As they reached the tree, the pirates halted.They were shocked to see what they saw. The ground had been dug up, though not recently: grass had begun to **sprout** in the hole. Someone had found the treasure before them and it was gone!

### Glossary

- recap : to remember the past
- cheerily : happily
- disbelievingly : not believing one's own eyes
- rattled : worried
- marched : walked steadily
- extravagance : the practice of spending a lot of money, especially more than you should
- menacing : intended to threaten or frighten someone sprout beginning to grow

# 33 The Treasure Hunt—the Fall of a Chieftain

Everyone was **thunderstruck**: the pirates, including Silver, stood still as if unable to move. However, Silver was the first to get over the situation and start thinking about the next course of action. He kept a calm head, found his temper, and changed his plan before the others had had time to realize the disappointment.

He slyly slipped a pistol to Jim, asking to gear up for trouble, and began to quietly move away from the hollow spot creating a distance between the pirates on one side and Jim and himself on the other. Jim realized Silver had changed sides again and for good decided to be with Jim.

The pirates leapt into the hollow one after other, digging and trying their best to find any leftover treasure. Morgan salvaged all but one piece of gold. He shook it at Silver blaming him for this **predicament**. Merry too accused Silver of knowing it all along and leading them on. Silver made fun of them asking them to dig further if they wished to find nuts! The other pirates agreed with Merry and Morgan, and they all began to hurl curses and abuses at Silver.

There stood the four pirates on one side (Dick was left behind due to his illness) and Jim and Silver on the other, with the pit in between.

At last, Merry began to make a speech, taking on his role of new captain. Suddenly Silver fired a shot into Merry's body and he fell dead into the pit. Immediately, the three others turned and ran away.

Meanwhile, at the same moment Dr Livesey, Gray, and Ben Gunn appeared from behind the nearby trees with pistols in their hands. The doctor commanded everyone to follow the pirates to chase them away from the small boats left near an inlet. After pursuing them through the woods, they realized that the pirates had headed in the opposite direction, towards Mizzenmast Hill. Gunn and Silver greeted each other, and the group proceeded down-hill, as Gunn related the long tale. Silver thanked the doctor for coming for him and Jim.

It turned out that it was Ben Gunn who first found the skeleton pointer and figured out where the treasure was. Ben Gunn carried all the gold from the treasure chests to his cave two months before the *Hispaniola* even arrived on the island. Gunn gave out this secret to Dr. Livesey on the night of the attack. The doctor on finding the anchorage **deserted** the next morning gave Long John Silver the treasure map, which was no use any longer since the treasure had already been moved. Doctor Livesey explained why they gave up the fort to the pirates: Ben Gunn had plenty of salted goat meat stored away, so the doctor and his friends could very well survive without the supplies they had brought. Also, Dr. Livesey thought it wasn't safe to stay at the fort with its marshland and the possibility of malaria.

The doctor admitted that he felt bad to leave Jim to his fate, but he had to do what was best for the people who had stuck to their duties, and unfortunately Jim hadn't.

That morning, when the doctor found out that Jim was back at the pirates' camp and might be in danger, he took Gray and Gunn across the island to lie in wait. It was Gunn's idea to play with his fellow pirates' **superstitions** and it worked too. Silver agreed that he was lucky that Jim was there; otherwise the pirates would have killed Silver, too, without a thought. Dr. Livesey agreed too.

By this time the group had reached the boats. The doctor destroyed one of them with a pick-axe and they all set sail in the other. They were soon**skimming** swiftly over a smooth sea. Passing around the hill, they caught sight of the Squire waiting outside Gunn's cave. Three miles farther, they found the *Hispaniola*, cruising by herself.After a sight of the ship, they pulled back again around the cave and dropped anchor. They climbed to the cave.

Jim was surprised as the Squiremet him most kindly, without even mentioning his escapade. However, the Squire was not very pleased to see Silver. He told Silver that although the Squire had been told not to **prosecute** Silver, the fact remains that he was a villain and an impostor, who deserved all the blame and guilt for the men who had died. When Silver thanked him, the Squire cried that this was against his duty, and not something he should be thanked for.

Ben Gunn's cave was a large, airy place, with a little spring and a pool of clear water, overhung with ferns. The floor was sand. Captain Smollett laid in one of the corners resting, and in another far corner there was great heaps of coin and bars of gold. That was Flint's treasure that the party had come so far to seek and that had cost the lives of seventeen men from the *Hispaniola,* and many more in the past.

Captain Smollett was happy to see Jim as well. He said that Jim had acted cleverly, however, the Captain and Jim should never sail together again as their views did not match. The Captain asked Silver why he was back, to which Silver replied that he was back at duty.

They all have a hearty meal that night with Ben Gunn's salted goat and some delicacies and a bottle of old wine from the *Hispaniola*. Silver too enjoyed the feast but remained at a slight distance from the rest, acting like the same **bland** and polite sailor who had begun the trip with them. Everyone was happy.

## Glossary

- thunderstruck : shocked beyond belief
- predicament : a difficult or unpleasant situation that is not easy to get out of
- deserted : left alone
- superstitions : a belief that things such as magic or luck have the power to affect your life
- skimming : move quickly over a surface
- prosecute : to officially accuse someone of a crime and ask a court of law to judge them
- bland : boring`

# 34 And Last

The group spent the next few days carrying the huge of mass treasure from the cave to the ship, in several rounds. It was a considerable task for so small a number of workmen. One person kept a watch at all times looking out for any attack by the three pirates. However, not much was seen of those three mutineers since that day. Gray and Ben Gunn came and went with the boat, while the rest **piled** the treasure on the beach. Jim was assigned the task of sorted all the money into bread-bags. Jim enjoyed this job greatly as it was a strange collection of coins covering almost all the currencies of the world.

A few days later, on one of the nights Dr. Livesey and Jim heard some strange shrieking and singing, while out on a stroll. The doctor knew at once that it was the mutineers. Silver remarked that they sounded drunk. The doctor felt that they might be sick. Bound by his medical duties, he thought of reaching out to them with help. Silver cautioned the doctor, saying if he did that he wouldn't return alive. Later, on another occasion they heard a gunshot far away, and supposed the men were hunting.

Jim noticed that the three older men treated Silver with the slightest regard. However, Silver did not seem to mind the **snide** behaviour and treated them with utmost respect and friendliness. Jim, however, felt a sense of **gratitude** towards him and Ben Gunn was still afraid of him for some reason.

It was decided that the mutineers would be abandoned on the island. The generous party left them some supplies for survival: a good stock of powder and shot, the bulk of the salt goat, a few medicines, and some other necessities such as tools, clothing, a spare sail, some rope, and by the particular desire of the doctor, a handsome present of tobacco. This deal seemed in many ways better than what awaited them back in England: the gallows.

The ship was stocked with enough water and the remainder of the goat meat and at last, one fine morning, the anchor was pulled up and the group set sail. As the ship began to pass, the three men were seen on the shore, kneeling and begging for forgiveness and to be taken along. While this did arouse some pity, the group decided to stay resolute on their decision of leaving them behind. The kind doctor waved at them and pointed to where the supplies were. But they hardly paid attention.

At last, realizing that the ship wasn't stopping for them, one of the men took a shot at Silver, but missed. The party kept under cover for a while after that and soon the mutineers as well as the highest rock of the Treasure Island were out of sight. The ship needed a new set of crew to make it till home. So they made for the nearest port. They anchored at a port where Mexican Indians and black people were selling sweet-smelling fruits and vegetables. Squire Trelawney, Dr. Livesey, and Jim go ashore for a night on the town to **recover** from their long, hard stay on the Treasure Island and to hire a bunch of fresh crewmen. When they returned to the *Hispaniola* at sundown, Ben Gunn had a piece of news for them: Silver had made an escape. He had not gone empty-handed though, he took along one of the coin sacks worth three or four hundred **guineas**. Everyone seemed pleased at this arrangement and felt that it was a cheap price to be rid of him.

Ben Gunn was on deck alone, and as soon as we came on board he began, with wonderful contortions, to make us a confession. Silver was gone. The maroon had connived at his escape in a shore boat some hours ago, and he now assured us he had only done so to preserve our lives, which would certainly have been forfeit if "that man with the one leg had stayed aboard." But this was not all. The sea-cook had not gone empty-handed. He had cut through a bulkhead unobserved and had removed one of the sacks of coin, worth perhaps three or four hundred guineas, to help him on his further wanderings.

After that, the *Hispaniola* had a safe voyage back home, although only five men of all those had sailed returned. The treasure was shared amply between those that returned, and each spent the money differently. Captain Smollett retired from the sea. Gray saved his money, studied his profession and became the owner of a ship besides starting a family. Ben Gunn spent all his money in just three weeks and was back to begging soon. No one heard of Silver again, but Jim thought he must have met his wife and they were living comfortably somewhere.

Jim concluded his tale by saying that there is treasure still lying on the island - silver and weapons - but he would return to that island for any price. Indeed, the worst dreams he had were of the waves crashing on the island's coasts and the parrot Captain Flint saying, "Pieces of eight! Pieces of eight!"

### Glossary

- piled : to put a large number of things on top of each other
- snide : deliberately unkind in an indirect way
- gratitude : a feeling of being grateful to someone because they have given you something or have done something for you
- recover : to stop being affected by an unpleasant experience
- guineas : a unit of money or a gold coin used in Britain in the past

# Self Assessment

## Short Answers

1. What according to Silver were Dr. Livesey's and Captain Smollett's opinions about Jim, post his escapade?
2. What did the pirates hand over to Silver?
3. What had the pirates used to prepare the black spot?
4. Who gave the treasure map to Silver?
5. What news did Silver have for the doctor?
6. What did Dr. Livesey request for when he learned that Jim was back?
7. What did the doctor advise Silver?
8. How was Jim escorted out of the stockade when the pirates launched their treasure hunt?
9. What was the first shock that awaited the pirates on their treasure hunt?
10. Why were the pirates disheartened after seeing the human skeleton?
11. Who was scaring the pirates by impersonating Flint's voice?
12. Who among the pirates was scared even after the truth about dead Flint's voice was out?
13. What did the pirates see where the treasure was supposed to be?
14. What was Jim asked to do with the treasure?
15. Even long after the expedition ended, what were Jim's worst dreams about?

## Comprehension

1. Describe what Jim saw in the stockade.
2. How did the pirates acquire the stockade and the supplies?
3. What did Jim reveal to the mutineers about himself in his speech?

4. Why did Silver want to make a deal with Jim? What was his deal?
5. How did Silver respond to the pirates' complaints about him?
6. Describe briefly the conversation between Jim and Dr. Livesey when they met outside the stockade?
7. How did Silver mislead the pirates about them having a upper hand in the game?
8. Why was Jim suspicious of Silver's intentions even after they made a deal?
9. What did Silver deduce about the human skeleton?
10. What had happened to the treasure?
11. Why had Dr. Livesey and his group given the treasure map to Silver and left the stockade as well?
12. What did the group decide to do with the three remaining mutineers?
13. What was Silver's final fate?

## Grammar

1. Classify these sentences as simple, compound, and complex.
   (a) The rest of the day passed away quietly.

   ______________

   (b) Silver seated himself across the room and began to fill a pipe.

   ______________

   (c) Silver was against killing Jim because they could be used as a hostage to make a deal.

   ______________

   (d) Silver seemed a bit shaken at first, but he quickly brushed it off.

   ______________

   (e) The pirates were struck by horror it seemed.

   ______________

   (f) Dr. Livesey gave Long John Silver the treasure map, since the treasure had already been moved.

   ______________

(g) Jim was glad to hear the sound, yet his gladness was not without admixture.

_______________

(h) The next morning Jim was woken up by Dr. Livesey's voice.

_______________

(i) The pirates thought he heard Flint, although Silver reminded them that he was dead.

_______________

(j) The pirates had lost all courage and were not eager to carry on.

_______________

## Short Answers

1. Why does Jim begin to recount his adventures of the Treasure Island?
2. Who is the first pirate that Jim meets? Where?
3. Where was the Captain when a pale stranger came looking for him?
4. Who came to the inn on the day of Jim's father's funeral?
5. Jim saw two deaths in a week. Who all died?
6. Where did Jim and his mother flee for help?
7. Why was Jim searching the dead Captain's pockets?
8. How did Pew die?
9. Who accompanied Jim to Dr. Livesey's house after the pirates were caught? Who was the doctor with?
10. Where did Squire Trelawney go to acquire the ship?

## Comprehension

1. How would the Captain spend his time at Admiral Benbow?
2. '...there was enough mystery surrounding the Captain as well'. Name a few things which support this idea.
3. Describe the first encounter between Dr. Livesey and Captain Billy Bones.

4. How did the meeting between the Captain and Black Dog turn out?
5. What did the Captain disclose to Jim about Flint and his men?
6. What do you think the 'black spot' means?
7. Who handed over the 'black spot' to the Captain? What affect did it have on him?
8. Why did Jim and his mother decide to flee the inn?
9. What did Jim and his mother find in the Captain's chest?
10. Were the pirates sad to find the Captain dead? What do you think they were looking for?
11. What were the contents of the oil-skin packet that Jim acquired from the Captain's chest?
12. Why did Squire Trelawney want to obtain a ship? Who all were to sail with him?

## Grammar

I. Choose the correct meaning of the following phrases as used in the text.

1. Out-of-the-way
   a. a remote location
   b. try very hard to do something
   c. go out of sight
   d. off-route
2. ill-at-ease
   a. something easy
   b. uncomfortable
   c. relaxing
   d. fall ill
3. sprang to his feet
   a. stand up quickly
   b. start jumping
   c. something falls on the feet
   d. run away

4. jump in his skin
    a. dancing
    b. feel an itch
    c. being pinched
    d. strongly shocked
5. scared out of their wits
    a. be very frightened
    b. say something very witty
    c. play a prank
    d. burst out laughing
6. got the better of
    a. get the best possible option
    b. perform well
    c. to win over something else
    d. persuade someone
7. cared two hoots
    a. take care of something
    b. care about two hoots
    c. not care about something
    d. care a lot
8. out of harm's way
    a. to fail to harm someone
    b. reach a safe place
    c. a dangerous path
    d. someone's harmful ways
9. motley crew
    a. an odd group of people
    b. a ship's crew
    c. inmates of the inn
    d. police officers
10. silent as the grave
    a. be completely silent
    b. to break a promise
    c. a silent service for someone dead
    d. to keep quiet when near a grave

II. Given below are a few sentences from the story. State which part of speech the underlined words belong to.

1. Jim decides to record every detail of what took place, <u>but</u> omits the part about the island's exact location.
2. The <u>story</u> begins with Jim recounting his first meeting with an old sailor called Billy Bones.
3. His raucous drinking and coarse singing <u>often</u> frightened the other inmates.
4. Dr. Liveseycalmly predicted that death would be near if the Captain did not stop drinking.
5. On a <u>cold</u> January morning soon after, the Captain was out on a stroll along the beach.
6. <u>He</u> rushed back in, to witness a lively sword fight.
7. Jim and his mother <u>ran</u> to his rescue but in vain.
8. That night Jim's father, who had also been <u>gravely</u> ill, died.
9. The mother and son realized that the Captain had left them in a perilous <u>situation.</u>
10. Jim took a moment to <u>observe</u>Squire Trelawney closely.

## Activity

Complete this crossword with names of characters from the story.

*http://my.puzzle-maker.com/start?O=29a749g8uez0ekptHHaqiejm-Hdmmiqhsbu2Due&StartPuzzle=Untitled.cw*

Please use the online puzzle generator to create the grid. It's an original puzzle, all clues have been created to generate the grid.

Across
3 narrator of the story
5 part of the ship's crew
8 officer in command
9 the blind beggar
10 old sailor in Admiral Benbow

Down
1 Trelawney was a ____________
2 notorious dead pirate with lot of wealth

4 he brought the black spot
6 Mrs ________________ was Jim's mother
7 Dr ______________ treated Jim's father

## Short Answers

1. Why was Jim staying at the Squire's mansion?
2. What did Squire Trelawney do to act sailorly?
3. Where does Jim meet Silver for the first time?
4. At the tavern where Jim met Silver, he identified one other person. Who was it?
5. Who was Arrow?
6. What was Jim's opinion of Captain Smollett after the first meeting?
7. What was the name given to Silver by his friends?
8. Who were the two people Silver was conversing with near the apple barrel?
9. How did Jim slip out of the barrel?
10. What did Silver plan to do with the honest men once the treasure was found?

## Comprehension

1. What did Squire Trelawney's letter contain?
2. Describe Silver as seen by Jim for the first time.
3. What were the Captain's opinions about the ship and the crew?
4. The Captain suggested a few changes on the ship for the safety of the Squireand his men. What were these changes?
5. What was the first unusual thing to take place onboard the *Hispaniola*?
6. Who was Cap'n Flint? What does Silver tell Jim about him?
7. How did Jim get locked in the apple barrel?

8. What did Jim hear hidden in the apple barrel?
9. How does Silver describe the island when it is first spotted from the ship?
10. What was the terrible news that Jim was eager to share with Dr. Livesey and the others?
11. Why did the Captain say that they cannot turn the ship back, even after learning about Silver's true intentions?
12. According to Dr. Livesey, who could be helpful in extracting information from the pirates? Why?

## Grammar

1. Match these phrases to their meanings.

   sounded off

   watch out

   set off

   baited breath

   full swing

   stepped up

   settle down

   letting down
2. Rewrite the given paragraph from the story with proper punctuation (comma, full-stop and apostrophe) and capitalization. Look out for spelling errors as well

One fine day then a letter from the Squire arrived. originally addressed to Dr. Livesey, the letter also bore the permision for jim to open it in the doctor's absence the letter informed that Squiretrelawney had bought a schooner called *Hispaniola,* which was ready to sail. theSquire described his meeting with an old sailor a fellow named long john silver who had lost a leg in war the one-legged sailer missed the sea and wished to sail again. theSquire was touched by his story and hired him as the ships cook. silver in turn helped the Squire find a suitabal crew for the ship. Squiretrelawney desired jim and Dr. Livesey to join him forthwith in bristol.

## Short Answers

1. Squire Trelawney's servants were told about Silver's treachery. What were their names?
2. What creature did Jim meet on the island when he fled from the pirates?
3. What was Ben Gunn wearing when Jim met him?
4. What does "marooned" mean?
5. Ben Gunn promised to help Jim and his friends. What did he ask in return?
6. What had Ben Gunn built with his tools?

## Comprehension

1. What did the island look like from the ship?
2. Why did Captain Smollett decide to give a day-off to the crew?
3. Jim did something reckless. What did he do?
4. Describe what Jim saw when he explored the island on his own for the first time.
5. "He heard two voices, one of which he recognized was Silver's." What did Jim see and hear from his hiding?
6. Who did Jim meet when he ran from the pirates? Why was Jim unsure of his identity?
7. How was Ben Gunn left behind on the island?

## Grammar

1. Write one synonym and one antonym for each of these words.

| | SYNONYM | ANTONYM |
|---|---|---|
| (a) clear | ____________ | ____________ |
| (b) several | ____________ | ____________ |
| (c) screaming | ____________ | ____________ |
| (d) safe | ____________ | ____________ |

(e) delighted ______________ ______________

(f) honest ______________ ______________

(g) argument ______________ ______________

(h) bright ______________ ______________

(i) crazy ______________ ______________

(j) loyal ______________ ______________

1. Write the meaning of these expressions.

    (a) gloomy and grey

    ______________________________

    (b) taken into confidence

    ______________________________

    (c) reckless decision

    ______________________________

    (d) stick to duty

    ______________________________

    (e) taken aback

    ______________________________

## Short answers

1. Who informed Dr. Livesey and the rest that Jim was not on the ship?
2. What did Dr. Livesey find on the island?
3. Who among the mutineers was convinced to join the loyal men?
4. Who among the current group of pirates was Flint's gunman back in the day?
5. Who among the loyal men was shot, at the end of the first day's fighting?
6. "Captain Smollett had been busy unpacking all the stuff he brought along stuffed in his coat." What were these things?

7. How did Jim learn that his friends were at the stockade?
8. Dr. Livesey decided to take a piece of ________________ for Ben Gunn.
9. Jim and Captain Smollett were not great shooters. How were they supposed to help during the battle?

## Comprehension

1. Describe the stockade found by Dr. Livesey.
2. How did the doctor and his men go about the plan of setting themselves up at the stockade?
3. Why did Captain Smollett and the others decide to sink to jolly boat?
4. What did Ben Gunn make Jim promise him?
5. Captain Smollett assigned duties to everyone in the log house. What were everyone asked to do?
6. Describe in brief the conversation that took place between Captain Smollett and Silver on the morning of the attack.
7. What was the Captain's last offer to Silver?
8. How did Jim fight Job Anderson? Who killed Anderson?

## Grammar

1. Underline the prepositions in these sentences.
   (a) The stockade was located on top of a hill.
   (b) Hunter pulled a good oar and soon they were on the ship again.
   (c) The boat listed to and fro with the weight.
   (d) The men waded to the beach unharmed.
   (e) They each had a loaded pistol in their hands.

## Short answers

1. Why was Captain Smollett pinned to the bed for a few weeks after the attack?

2. Why did Jim decide to leave the stockade without telling anyone?
3. What did Jim do after he found the boat?
4. What kind of creatures did Jim see when his boat drifted away?
5. Why did Jim want to board the *Hispaniola*?
6. Which two pirates were on board when Jim reappeared on the *Hispaniola*?
7. What did Israel Hands request Jim to get him as soon as he saw him?
8. Why did Jim throw away the pirate's flag from the ship?
9. How did Jim learn that Hands was not as injured as he showed?
10. Why did Jim think Captain Smollett would forgive him?

## Comprehension

1. Why did Jim envy Dr. Livesey when he left the stockade?
2. Why did Jim want to leave the stockade? What was his plan?
3. Describe in brief how Jim set the Hispaniola free?
4. How did Jim board the Hispaniola?
5. What deal did Israel Hands strike with Jim?
6. How did Jim reclaim the Hispaniola? Describe briefly.
7. What happened when Jim entered the stockade?

## Grammar

1. Underline the adverbs in the following sentences.
   (a) The rest of the day passed away quietly.
   (b) Jim kept walking cautiously avoiding the anchorage.
   (c) The ship had started gliding swiftly through the water.
   (d) Finally Hands broke the silence.
   (e) Jim now knew that Israel Hands could move and he was armed.

2. Write sentences of your own using any five of these phrases.

   (a) looked after

   (b) heavily armed

   (c) got the better of him

   (d) peered through

   (e) to and fro

   (f) until further notice

   (g) keep an eye

   (h) pounced upon

# Summary

Jim Hawkins is a young boy who lives at his parents' inn, the Admiral Benbow, near Bristol, England, in the eighteenth century. An old sea captain named Billy Bones dies in the inn after being presented with a black spot, or official punishment for pirates. Jim is stirred to action after this incident. Jim and his mother find Billy Bone's sea chest and hastily unlock it to find a logbook and a treasure map inside. Hearing steps outside, they leave with the documents before Billy's enemies ransack the inn.

Jim realizes that the contents he has snatched from the sea chest must be valuable, so he takes one of the documents he has found to family friend Dr. Livesey and a local gentleman of fortune, Squire Trelawney. Excited, they recognize it as a map directing to a huge treasure that the infamous pirate Captain Flint has buried on a distant island. Squire Trelawney immediately starts planning an expedition to find the treasure. Inexperienced in his negotiations to prepare the ship for sail, Squire is tricked into hiring one of Flint's former mates, Long John Silver, and many of Flint's crew. Only the Captain of the ship, Captain Smollett, is trustworthy. The ship sets sail for Treasure Island. Everything seems fine, until Jim overhears Silver's plans for a mutiny. Jim tells the Captain about Silver and the rest of the rebellious crew.

Reaching the island, Captain Smollett thinks of a plan to get most of the mutineers off the ship by allowing them leisure time on shore. On a whim, Jim sneaks into the pirates' boat and goes ashore with them. Frightened of the pirates, Jim runs off alone. From a hiding place, he witnesses Silver murder a sailor who refuses to join the mutiny. Jim flees deeper into the heart of the island, where he encounters a half-crazy man named Ben Gunn. Ben had once served in Flint's crew but was marooned on the island three years ago.

Meanwhile, Captain Smollett and his men go ashore and take shelter in a stockade the pirates have built. Later, Jim returns to the stockade, bringing Ben with him. Silver visits the stockade soon after and attempts a negotiation with the Captain, but the Captain refuses to speak to him. The pirates attack the stockade the next day, and the Captain is wounded. Eager to take action, Jim makes another hasty decision. He secretly leaves the stockade, sneaking off to hunt for Ben's handmade boat hidden in the woods.

After finding Ben's boat, Jim sails out to the anchored ship with the intention of setting it sail, thereby depriving the pirates of a means of escape. He cuts the rope, but he realizes his small boat has drifted near the pirates' camp and fears he will be discovered. By chance, the pirates do not spot Jim, and he floats around the island until he catches sight of the ship drifting away. Struggling aboard, he discovers that one of the watchmen, Israel Hands, has killed the other watchman in a drunken fit. Jim takes control of the ship. But Israel Hands plans to attack him. In a deadly fight between the two, Jim is wounded but kills Israel.

Jim returns to the stockade but finds it occupied by the pirates. Silver takes Jim hostage, telling the boy that the Captain has given the pirates the treasure map, the supplies, and the use of the stockade in exchange for their lives. Jim realizes, however, that Silver is having trouble managing his men, who accuse him of treachery. Silver proposes to Jim that they help each other survive by pretending Jim is a hostage. However, the men present Silver with a black spot and inform him that they no longer consider him their commander.

In a desperate attempt to gain control of his crew, Silver shows them the treasure map to gain their trust. Silver leads Jim and the men to the treasure site, but they are shocked to find the treasure already gone. The men are angered and turn against Silver again. At that moment Dr. Livesey, Ben Gunn, and the others fire on the pirates, who run and scatter throughout the island. Jim and Silver flee, and are guided by the doctor and others to Ben's cave, where Ben has hidden the treasure. Ben had discovered the treasure months before.

After spending three days carrying the loot to the ship, the men prepare to set sail for home. The pirates are left marooned on the island. Silver is allowed to join the voyage, but he sneaks off the ship one night with a portion of the treasure and is never heard from again. The rest of the men reach home safely.